EVER SO ELIGIBLE

After several minutes  the tasks she had set he Olivia's mind returnd to

He really was a stubb

Very well, she thought, sitting up in the bed and lighting the candle on the table. She picked up a small notebook and opened it. Taking out the pencil tucked inside, she was ready to begin her list of eligible young ladies, suitable young ladies, young ladies worthy of the Marquess of Sheridan.

Five minutes later, Olivia set the pencil aside, staring in wonder at the words she had doodled while waiting for inspiration to strike.

Lady Olivia Sheridan.

Other novels by Julia Parks

THE DEVIL AND MISS WEBSTER

HIS SAVING GRACE

A GIFT FOR A ROGUE

TO MARRY AN HEIRESS

FORTUNE'S FOOLS

Published by Kensington Publishing Corp.

LADY OLIVIA
TO THE RESCUE

JULIA PARKS

ZEBRA BOOKS
KENSINGTON PUBLISHING CORP.
www.kensingtonbooks.com

ZEBRA BOOKS are published by

Kensington Publishing Corp.
850 Third Avenue
New York, NY 10022

All Kensington titles, imprints and distributed lines are available at special quantity discounts for bulk purchases for sales
promotion, premiums, fund-raising, educational or institutional
use.

Special book excerpts or customized printings can also be
created to fit specific needs. For details, write or phone the
office of the Kensington Special Sales Manager: Kensington
Publishing Corp., 850 Third Avenue, New York, NY 10022.
Attn. Special Sales Department. Phone: 1-800-221-2647.

Zebra and the Z logo Reg. U.S. Pat. & TM Off.

First Printing: February 2005
10 9 8 7 6 5 4 3 2 1

Printed in the United States of America

For my family—
Dennis, Stuart, Jamie and her David,
Tiffany and her David, Hallie, Truman,
and Amanda.

CHAPTER ONE

"And the name of that beauty?"

"That? Oh, what is the creature's name?" said the tall gentleman, frowning slightly as the beauty twirled by in the arms of a clumsy young man whose dress proclaimed him fresh from the country. The lady was smiling all the same, even as the young man landed squarely on her foot. *Serves her right for dancing with such a lout,* thought the elegant Lord Sheridan.

With a snap of his long fingers, he said, "Cunningham, that's it. Lady Olivia Cunningham."

"She fairly takes one's breath away," murmured Sir Richard Adair, a lascivious smile playing on his lips.

"Then by all means, dear fellow, do take her away," said his friend, turning away from the dancers, his nostrils flaring in disdain. "'Twould be a service to all, ridding London of one of its perpetually cheerful ornaments—full of beauty and void of rational thought."

"I say, Sheri, that's rather harsh, even for you," said his other companion, Lady Madeline Thorpe. "Everyone speaks very highly of Lady Olivia, though I do not know her personally."

A smile flickered in the eyes of the Marquess of Sheridan as he glanced down at his friend. "I daresay you and the beautiful Lady Olivia have not moved in the same select circles, Maddie. You are much too practical to be forever dancing the night away, smiling in that vapid fashion at whoever has asked for the pleasure of your company. Your conversation is much too articulate to be suited to the likes of a Lady Olivia."

"Sheridan," said the lady. She feigned shock, but her eyes were twinkling merrily. "Much too harsh, even for you."

"Yes, dear chap, one might even speculate that you have an interest in the lady," drawled Sir Richard. "The gentleman doth protest too much and all."

The Marquess of Sheridan raised his quizzing glass. Looking down his aquiline nose, he studied his friends a moment before allowing the glass to drop.

Turning back to the dancers, he said haughtily, "I would rather face the dogs of hell than spend a minute in conversation with a female the likes of Lady Olivia. Come, let us adjourn to the card room. At least there, I shall have the pleasure of fleecing the two of you of your purses."

"You know what they say, Sheri," said Sir Richard as he offered his arm to Lady Thorpe, patting her hand in a familiar fashion. "Lucky at cards, unlucky at love."

"Ah, and isn't that fortunate for me," said the

marquess, falling in step behind them. "If only my wife had guessed how very wealthy I would become at the tables, she might have put off dying a few more years."

Gurgling with laughter, Lady Thorpe said, "Sheri! That is too bad of you, even if you are the self-proclaimed leader of our little company of misanthropists! I mean, she was your late wife!"

"Who was as empty headed as most of this assemblage and twice as avaricious," he muttered. "I have often thought that Anne would somehow have survived if she had only known that I would be able to repair the family fortunes to the extent that I have done."

The dancers took no notice of the departure of the trio, save one beautiful young lady with golden hair and deep blue eyes. She could not help the rush of relief that flooded over her when those three most high and mighty turned to go. She had been aware of their scrutiny—the ball was hardly a crush, so it would have been impossible to remain ignorant of it—especially the handsome latecomer.

Lady Olivia was not accustomed to noticing the appearances of other people. She was far more interested in the inner person, but the handsome Lord Sheridan was impossible to overlook. His dark hair, silvering at the temples, was always groomed to perfection. His figure was as slim as that of a youth, and yet, there was something very powerful about the manner in which he carried himself. Perhaps it was the way he had of staring through that silver-rimmed quizzing glass. There was also that cane that he carried everywhere he went. That he would bring a cane to a ball and not give it up to the care of the servants bespoke an arrogance about him. It was as if he wanted to proclaim to all that he had no intention of dancing, of joining the fun. He was present merely as an observer, looking down that aquiline nose at the entire company.

"I say, my lady, have I done something to annoy you?" asked the nervous youth who presently held her in his arms.

Olivia laughed, setting him at his ease. "Certainly not, Mr. Campion. I'm afraid I was woolgathering. I do beg your pardon."

This was said with such a perfect smile that the young man blushed to the roots of his hair and stammered, "There . . . that is . . . no need, I'm sure. Did that man staring at you upset you?"

"I hadn't really noticed. I was wondering who Lord Sheridan's new friend might be," she lied.

"I'm afraid I don't even know Lord Sheridan, but I did notice that he was staring at you . . . not that I blame him."

Ignoring the young man's attempt at gallantry, Olivia said, "Oh, then you will not have remarked on the presence of his friend, a man I have not seen before. I know it is silly of me," she said with a beguiling giggle. "But I do pride myself on knowing absolutely everyone in the *ton*. Lord Sheridan's friend, his gentleman friend that is, is a stranger to me."

"If you like, my lady, I will inquire after we finish our dance."

"No, that is not at all necessary. I shall find out in the course of the evening," she said, wincing when he trod on her foot yet again. She protested at his apology, assuring him that it had been a glancing blow.

Olivia welcomed the final chord of music, taking the young man's arm for a promenade around the room. She saw her Aunt Amy in the midst of a group of like-minded older women, enjoying a comfortable gossip, and insisted that she had to speak to her immediately. Allowing Mr. Campion to bow over her hand and give it an awkward kiss, she sailed into the gathering of gossipmongers and took the chair beside her aunt with a sigh of relief.

Before Olivia could open her mouth, her aunt said, "I don't believe you have met Mrs. Campion, my dear, the mother of the young man you just took a turn with about the dance floor."

Olivia smiled and greeted the other woman warmly while she gave her aunt's arm a grateful squeeze.

Someone else claimed Mrs. Campion's attention, and Olivia whispered, "Thank you, Aunt. I was about to mention how my feet are aching. What a *faux pas* that would have been."

Her lively aunt chuckled and said, "What a delightful pun, my dear. A *false step* indeed! I would say her son is more than accomplished at the *faux pas!*"

"Shh, she will hear you," whispered Olivia, managing to contain her own amusement with difficulty. "And aside from his very large feet, Mr. Campion is a charming gentleman," she finished as the young man's mother turned to smile at her broadly.

"Oh, I told Percy that he would have to be careful here in London. I warned him that he would be so very popular with the young ladies that he mustn't allow it to go to his head," said the matron.

"Or his feet," whispered Olivia's incorrigible aunt.

Mrs. Campion was oblivious, however, as she warmed to her favorite theme. "Dear Percy is unaccustomed to a great deal of feminine company, you know. He is only lately home from Cambridge."

"Yes, he was telling me as much," murmured Olivia politely.

Hearing the rather dull story of Percy Campion's four and twenty years had been bad enough the first time. She did not wish to relive the tale through his mother's doting eyes.

"He should have liked to remain in the world of scholars, but his father needed him at home," said the matron.

"Yes, I can quite understand that," said Olivia, rising as she spoke. "If you will excuse me, I see my next partner approaching."

As she hurried away, she heard Mrs. Campion continue, "Our estate is so large, you see. . . ."

Poor Aunt Amy, thought Olivia. She swept a curtsey as the handsome Lord Hardcastle bowed before her. He took her hand to help her rise and tucked it proprietorially into the crook of his arm. She gave his arm a squeeze and smiled up at him.

A prickling on the back of her neck caused her to glance across the room. She almost gasped when her eyes met the coal-black gaze of the Marquess of Sheridan standing on the other side of the crowded ballroom. He gave a slight nod. This small acknowledgement made the blood rush to her cheeks, and Olivia looked away, grateful to return to the comfortable face of her old friend.

"Something wrong?" asked Lord Hardcastle, patting her hand.

"Wrong?"

Her voice was breathless—as if she had just been kissed. To clear her head, she shook it in response. What in the world was the matter with her? She had been on the Town for years! She was hardly a green miss to be swept away by a mere glance!

"Have you seen her?"

Olivia had to force herself to attend her partner as he took her into his arms. Her eyes followed the direction of his nod, and she smiled, glad for the diversion.

"Yes, I think Miss Featherstone is even lovelier tonight than usual. I did suggest that color of yellow might suit her when we chanced to meet at the dressmakers."

"Bravo," said Tony, grinning at her. "I know you think she is merely the latest in my long line of infatuations, but I believe I have finally found the future Lady Hardcastle."

"Really, Tony? Oh, that is marvelous! I am so glad I thought to introduce you to her." Then Olivia sighed.

"Whatever is the matter? Are you not the one who told me I was only in love with love and not with the woman—namely you? Do not tell me you have changed your mind and want to reconsider my offer after all these years."

"Certainly not, and yes, I did say all that then, and I still mean it now," she replied, her blue eyes twinkling.

"And you were right at the time, but I have waited long enough. I am almost thirty years old, Olivia. I can't be racketing about London forever. It is time I took a wife."

With his chest puffed out and his brow creased, he looked so very serious, her dear old friend. She could not bear to lose him, as she inevitably would when he married. Olivia felt tears prickling her eyes, and she quickly bowed her head to regain her composure. How selfish of her! If she couldn't love Tony the way he deserved to be loved, at least she loved him enough to wish him happy.

When she looked up, she said sensibly, "Of course you should take a wife, Tony, and I think Miss Featherstone will make you a wonderful wife. And I know she is very fond of you. She confided as much to me herself."

"Really?"

His boyish expression brought a smile to Olivia's lips and she nodded. "You should speak to her father soon, though. She is such a sweet girl, I cannot believe she will not receive other offers."

He stopped cold, and Olivia had to drag him through the next few steps as she hissed, "Not now, stupid. It can wait until tomorrow." As he again fell into the steps of the waltz, she added, "Heaven save me from people in love!"

They laughed comfortably. She listened with half an ear, inserting a comment now and again, as he rehearsed his speech for Lord Featherstone and then, if all went well, for the beautiful Miss Featherstone.

At the end of their waltz, Olivia passed to her next partner, until the evening had turned to morning and it was time to say her farewells.

Arm in arm with her aunt, they passed the card room when a shout of triumph claimed their attention.

"I told you I would beat you tonight!"

"How intuitive of you," came the dry reply.

The music from the ballroom rose in a crescendo as the speaker reached the doorway. Looking over his shoulder and bidding the unseen victor a hearty good night, Lord Sheridan raised his silver-handled cane in farewell, or defiance.

With a jaunty twist, it descended, glancing off Olivia's shoulder, causing her to yelp. Caught off guard, she tripped over her own feet and had to clutch her aunt's arm to steady herself.

Strong hands grasped her around the waist.

Olivia let out another yelp as the cane landed on her foot. Hopping on her good foot, she looked into the eyes of her tormentor and savior and proceeded to choke. Blue eyes streaming with tears, she gasped for breath while her helpful aunt pounded her back, robbing her of air.

After what seemed like hours, while the crowd gathered, Olivia managed to regain her breath and most of her composure. Silent laughter, however, masked her recovery, and she found it impossible to stop.

"I beg your pardon, Lady Olivia, isn't it?"

She nodded.

"Let me carry you to . . ." She fended off the handsome Lord Sheridan with a wave of her hand. "I should have been watching where I was going."

Olivia appeared to nod in agreement as she threw back her head, took a gulp of air, and leaned forward again, beginning to laugh out loud. He frowned fiercely, his manner changing in an instant from apologetic to affronted.

As he stepped away from her, she clutched at his coat and shook her head. While he pried loose her fingers, she finally managed, "I am not really injured, my lord. Only laughing at the absurdity of the situation. Please, do not take offense."

She saw his dark eyes change in a flash from ice to warmth. He smiled at her, and Olivia almost gasped at the magnetism of his expression. She had never before seen the cynical Lord Sheridan smile with anything but disdain, a mere curling of the lip. But this was different. Then the warmth was gone, and she wondered if she had merely imagined it.

In the bustle of regaining her dignity and composure, of smoothing her gown while he collected his fallen cane, and of assuring her aunt that she was fine and no longer in need of having her back assaulted, the moment of intimacy was completely erased. With a courteous bow from Lord Sheridan and a slight curtsey from Olivia, they parted company.

Olivia was quiet all the way home. When her maid had dressed her in her nightrail, she wandered around the elegantly appointed bedchamber for several minutes.

Finally, she climbed into bed.

While she had regained her optimistic outlook after that embarrassing episode, she reflected that it really was a shame that the Marquess of Sheridan was such a gloomy sort of fellow. He was always frowning despite the fact that he attended balls, routs, and even picnics—and despite the fact that he had such a wondrous smile. Though she hadn't given him much thought before, she had occasionally wondered why he bothered.

Tonight, however, she had glimpsed a different Lord Sheridan. Perhaps there had been a time, before his wife died in childbirth, that he had been a different sort of man. Perhaps he had been quite jolly.

This thought made Olivia chuckle, and she leaned over to blow out the candle. What an absurd image she had in her head. Lord Sheridan laughing gaily and capering around the dance floor. How ridiculous!

Her raggedy little cat hopped on the bed and found her hand, butting his head against it until she began to pet him.

"Yes, I know you are tired from your nightly wandering. So am I. That must be why I cannot settle my mind and go to sleep."

"Meow," said Hawkeye, turning over on his back and batting at her fingers.

Scratching his chin, her thoughts returned to the handsome marquess. She must have seen him at dozens of balls over the years, but she had never even seen him dance! Perhaps he simply did not know how. No, that was ridiculous.

Still, he must attend them for some reason.

Sighing, Olivia shut her eyes and resolved that

she would have to look into this matter of Lord Sheridan. Perhaps he needed her help. After all, it was not just the poor who needed a helping hand. Lord Sheridan was rumored to be as rich as Croesus, but he might still welcome some happiness into his dull life, and happiness was her specialty.

"What do you say, my lord? Should I send this H. Pelham a bank draft?"

"No, wait until Butters has a chance to check out his story. Go to Bow Street and see Butters at once."

"Very good, my lord. And the others?"

"Send them the usual—except that Mrs. Turner. Since the losses at Waterloo last year, the number of soldiers' widows has risen terribly. They deserve better than to be forgotten. Oh, and the vicar at home. Don't forget him. He's distributing the funds to the soldiers."

"Really, my lord, I believe giving the men and their families roofs over their heads should be quite sufficient," protested the marquess's secretary.

Drew grinned at the young man and shook his head. "Getting stingy with my money?"

"Oh, no, my lord, I would never presume. . . ."

"I know, Fitz, my boy. I was only making a small joke. I appreciate your careful marshalling of my affairs. You do a capital job. With you in charge, I never worry about any of my business concerns."

"Thank you, my lord," said the conscientious Mr. Fitzsimmons, blushing a fiery red.

"Then you will send the widow and the vicar twice what we normally do."

"Very good, my lord," said the young man, sitting down behind the desk once more as his employer turned and walked to the door.

The secretary popped up again when the marquess paused and turned. With that rare smile, the marquess said, "Only do send them a note saying that this is not a permanent increase."

"Certainly, my lord."

"Oh, and one more thing. Send some flowers to a Lady Olivia Cunningham. I don't know her address. Enclose a note saying that I hope she has suffered no lasting harm from our encounter, etc."

"Immediately, my lord." The secretary removed his spectacles and stepped around the desk.

The marquess grinned and said, "It is not as urgent as all that, Fitz. Anytime this morning will do."

"Oh, I thought . . ."

"No, no. Nothing of the sort. I dropped my cane, and it sort of landed on the lady. No doubt the bird-witted creature has already forgotten the incident, but I won't have it said that I do not know how to behave in polite society."

"Certainly not, my lord." The secretary returned to his chair, waiting patiently for his master to depart.

With a wave, Drew Benton, the Marquess of Sheridan, picked up his cane—today it was the one with the hand-carved lion's head—and made his way down the hall. The footman threw open the front door, bowing slightly when his master thanked him.

Gratified to see the blue sky peeking through the clouds, Drew hummed a little ditty under his breath as he strolled along the pavement. He walked from his house through the busy London streets to Hyde Park. It was not yet noon, and the park was quiet, another fact that lightened his usual gloomy expression.

His daughter had once asked him why he never smiled, and he had replied with a smile, but she had not been satisfied. Her childish goal had then become to make him smile at every encounter—at least once—and she had succeeded. The princess, as he affectionately termed her, would always get her way, if her father had any say in the matter. But the summer had ended. Rebekah had gone away to school for the first time, and when she returned, she was no longer his impish little girl. The Rebekah who had worked so hard to make him smile had changed into a serious young lady, one who had no time to make her father smile.

But she was a beauty! As beautiful as her mother, though he hoped her nature would make her kinder than his late wife had been. He supposed only time would tell.

Drew sat down on a bench. Sitting back, he scratched his chin with the cold ivory handle of his cane. He put down the cane, leaning it against the wooden bench.

And then there was Arthur, his heir. There had never been any camaraderie between them. The boy was bookish. He hated riding and shooting and fishing—all the things his father loved. He preferred living through the characters in his storybooks. His classes at Eton were easy for him. Living with other boys was proving much more difficult.

Still, it had been a month since Drew had received another wrenching letter, begging his father to allow him to go home and be tutored privately. Drew wondered every day if he had made the right decision, forcing the boy to remain at school. Perhaps this time, his decision had been for the best.

Drew sighed. Children really should come with directions. If truth be told, he knew nothing about them, and without a wife to help, he floundered around most of the time until hitting upon some solution to whatever problem they happened to present. It was hardly an efficacious way to go about the business of rearing one's offspring.

A young lady trotted by on her pony, eyeing him out of the corner of her eye. Her groom followed on another pony at a respectful distance. The young lady turned to see if Drew was watching her. He grimaced. Even though she was probably only a year or two older than his own daughter, she was sizing him up, trying to decide if he was marriage material.

Blast! What a dreadful thing this was, this thing called the Season. And here he was, joining in, more or less, just to keep up his contacts so that his own princess could have her Season when it came to her turn.

The thought of her . . . but there he was again. Thinking about his daughter becoming one of those young ladies. He had promised himself he would not, but it was becoming more and more difficult each year, as Rebekah grew another year closer to it.

Whatever had happened to those ivory towers where a fellow could lock up his damsel and keep her to himself? With another grimace, he rose and stretched. Even if he had a tower, it wouldn't be strong enough to hold Rebekah. She was as stubborn as her father, he thought with pride. Besides, all she would have to do to secure her release would be to turn those soulful brown eyes on him and say please. Her doting father would be lost instantly.

Drew glanced up at the cloudy sky. The sun had disappeared, and dark clouds loomed in the distance. He returned to the gates of the park and waited for a break in the carriages before crossing the pavement. Finally, he made his way to his club where he discovered Sir Richard consuming a huge meal.

"Have a seat, Drew. Another plate," he called to the waiter, but Drew waved the servant away.

His friend shrugged and said, "I don't know how you can deny yourself. That beggarly supper buffet at Lady Pinchot's last night has worn completely away."

When this complaint brought no response, Sir Richard laid his fork on the table and studied his friend.

"I say, Drew, you're looking particularly glum today."

"No more than usual. I was thinking of Rebekah and the fact that in only a year—or two, if I can put her off that long—she will be making her bow into Society. I cannot like the idea."

"No father likes it, I believe. Can you not leave that to your mother?"

"My mother? Do you not remember my mother? She is the one who never leaves the country, never comes to Town. Why the devil do you think I am here? All my mother does is tell me I had better come to Town and keep up my contacts in Society if I want Rebekah to have a successful Season. My mother certainly has no intention of helping. So here I am, attending every demmed ball and rout for the past two years, trying to pave the way for my daughter. What I really want is to lock her in her room and bar the door to every jackanapes who so much as looks at her!"

"Fascinating," murmured his friend. "I had no idea fathers felt that way. Not that it would have changed my, uh, habits. But never mind about me."

"It is your sort who makes me want to lock her up and throw away the key," said Drew, signaling to the waiter to bring another glass.

"True, but you cannot lock her up. Granted, I have no experience in this matter, but I would imagine that it is rather like taking one's favorite horse to Tattersall's and putting him on the block. Not a joyous occasion. I mean, you know you want to sell the beast. That is what you have brought him there for, but when someone has bought the nag, another part of you wants very much to draw the fellow's cork."

Drew chuckled and nodded. "Though I think most ladies would be revolted by your analogy, I think it quite suitable. The thought of some young puppy coming to me and asking my permission to court my daughter . . . it makes me quite blue-deviled."

The waiter brought another glass, and Drew picked up his friend's bottle of wine and filled the glass to the top.

Raising it, Drew said heartily, "To our ladies and

our horses, the two things a gentleman values the
most."

"Here! Here!" said Sir Richard, lifting his glass
to his lips.

CHAPTER TWO

Poking her head into her aunt's chamber, Olivia said, "Aunt Amy, after I have done my other errands, I am going out to the shops. Might I bring you something?"

"No, I don't think so, m'dear," said the older woman from her bed where she sipped her chocolate. "Nothing I can think of so early in the day."

"But it is one o'clock in the afternoon," protested Olivia with a laugh.

"Precisely, and after seeking my bed at four o'clock this morning, it is much too early for the serious contemplation of shopping." The older woman put out her hand and picked up a pair of spectacles from the bedside table. Eyeing her niece, she said, "Going to the shops dressed like that?"

Olivia glanced down at her modestly cut navy blue gown and said, "I see nothing wrong with it. Would you prefer I wear silks and satins when I visit the poor?"

"Do not be absurd, child. No, but you are going to the shops, too."

"Yes, but I am not attending the opera or a ball, and if I happen to meet any of my friends, they will simply have to take me as they see me—which I'm sure they will."

"You sometimes place too much faith in people's judgement," commented her aunt as she removed the spectacles.

"So, you still cannot think of anything you need?" asked Olivia.

"No, no, you run along, but do take Harold and your maid with you. My qualms about your fashion sense aside, one can never be too careful of one's reputation, my dear."

"Pansy has caught a chill, so I have ordered her to bed for the day, but you know I never go anywhere without Harold. Rest well, dear Aunt."

Olivia closed the door as her aunt intoned, "A husband would be much more suitable company."

Chuckling, Olivia padded silently along the carpeted corridor of her town house and tripped down the steps to the front door.

The butler appeared, and she spent several minutes consulting with him before leaving the house. Outside, the coachman on the box tipped his hat when she appeared.

"Good morning, Mr. Pate. I hope the threatening rain does not trouble your rheumatism too much."

"Not too much, my lady. Thank you. And th' rain will wait until tonight, I think."

"Let us hope you are right."

"Will it be the usual round today?"

"Yes, but I want to begin with the widows' home so that we may deliver those boxes."

"Very good, my lady."

She stepped to the rear of the carriage where a small, wizened face appeared, grinning from ear to ear.

"How are you today, Rattle?"

"I'm just fine, bless you, m'lady," said the youth. "The good Lord is in his heaven. All's right with the world. Amen."

"Yes, well, thank you, Rattle."

Olivia then turned her smile on the huge servant by the carriage door, waiting patiently to hand her inside. When she was settled on the forward-facing seat, he climbed inside, too, taking the rear-facing seat opposite hers.

"How are you today, Harold?"

"I'm very well, thank you, m'lady," he replied with grave formality in his curiously high-pitched voice.

"How is Rattle faring?"

"He's fine. He likes workin' in th' stables, and since he found religion, he spends most of his spare time helping out at th' church."

With a chuckle, Olivia said, "Who would have thought a climbing boy named Rat would ever have changed to this extent?" As the carriage lurched forward, she added, "You may begin."

The large man removed a small book from his pocket and began to read. "The king look . . . ed, looked at his son and said, 'Let me he . . . luh . . . lip . . . he lip'?"

Olivia leaned across and glanced at the book. Hiding her amusement, she said, "Help. All the letters run together, you see."

"Help," the giant echoed. "Let me help you with your suh . . . kuh . . . crown."

Olivia listened with half an ear as her servant continued his lesson. She was pleased with Harold's progress. He was proving an apt pupil. If only the children would work as hard as he did.

Silence answered this unspoken thought, and she glanced up in surprise. Harold was looking out the window with a puzzled frown on his face.

"Oh, I forgot to tell you," she said. "We are going to end with the school today. Don't worry. I didn't forget that you are going to teach the children a new letter today."

He smiled, his gaping teeth lending his face a rather frightening aspect, but the faded blue eyes peering over his misshapen nose were tender.

"I am teaching them the letter *f* today, my lady."

"And what words are you going to use for that?" she asked.

Harold's background as a prizefighter had led him to use several colorful words to illustrate the letter *b*—*belting*, *bruiser*, and *bung*. The boys had loved his demonstrations, but the headmistress of their little school had been horrified and threatened to leave if Harold ever used similar words in her presence. Secretly, Olivia had thought him rather resourceful. After all, the former boxer had held the small group of restless boys mesmerized as he playacted hitting his opponents, bruising them, and "bunging their peepholes" shut.

From then on, the boys had clamored for more, but after Olivia's protests on behalf of the head-mistress, Harold had steadfastly refused to humor them. He had spit on his palm and pressed it to his heart when swearing that he would not break his word to his mistress, and he had not. For all that Harold Hanson had led a colorful life, he was a man of honor.

"I thought I would use *funny, farmer,* and if you think Mrs. Priddy wouldn't object, *fighter,* because I was one."

"I think that is perfectly acceptable as long as your playacting does not become too, uh, real."

"Oh, no, my lady. I'll be ever so polite about it."

"Then those words should all be fine, Harold. I'm very pleased that you are teaching those young scamps their letters. The girls don't seem to mind sitting down and learning, but the boys are much more active."

"They're just full of fun, my lady. They're not sweet like those little girls. Most of them boys lived too long working hard just to get by. It makes them restless to have everything given to them."

Olivia frowned. "Yes, it is a problem. I am glad you suggested that the children should make themselves useful around the school by doing chores. I was going to hire more maids, but I think your idea was better for everyone concerned."

The big man beamed at this praise. The carriage came to a stop before a dark brick building. The servant opened the door and jumped down, glancing around him before reaching his hand up to help his mistress descend. When she was safe inside, he returned to the carriage where Rattle had opened the boot. Loading their arms with boxes, they brought them inside, too.

"Here they are, Mr. Mullins. I think the ladies will find plenty to keep them busy," said Lady Olivia when Harold and her tiger entered, the boxes stacked so high they could barely see over them.

"Why don't we take the boxes into the workroom?" said Mr. Mullins. A man of medium height, his bearing was as crisp as the uniform he had once worn. With a sweep of his arm, he ushered Olivia through a dark hallway and up a narrow flight of stairs.

"How is old Mrs. Arvin doing?"

"She is still quite ill, I'm afraid. Her granddaughter is sitting with her. We cannot get her to eat anything, and the doctor holds out little hope."

"I am sorry to hear that. I will stop in to see her before I leave."

The reserved man pushed open a door to a spacious room filled with sunlight. The ladies looked up from their chairs and nodded, but they didn't rise. After several months, Olivia had finally been able to persuade them that this act of servitude was not required. She proceeded around the room, speaking to each woman by name, putting her hand on a shoulder here and admiring their handiwork there.

At the end of her promenade, she announced, "As always, your work is amazing, ladies. You will be pleased to know that your little business is becoming quite self-sufficient. Harold and I have brought you more clothes to remake and something extra, too."

She signaled to her servant, and he put the largest box on the table in the center of the room and popped it open. "Oohs" and "ahhs" rippled through the spacious workroom. Several of the older women left their seats and came forward to lift the lengths of fabric to their cheeks in appreciation.

"They are beautiful, my lady. Such fine fabrics I never have seen," said one of the women.

"They are that. The lengths of cloth are not new, but they have never been used. One of my acquaintances discovered all of these wonderful fabrics in some attic trunks. She had no use for them and thought of you. She has been very generous in the past, but as I told her, this donation is nothing short of a treasure."

"What do you want us to do with them, my lady?"

"You must decide that for yourselves, ladies. I have also brought some of the latest copies of Ackerman's fashion plates for you to study. Or perhaps you prefer to make children's garments. Mr. Mullins will help you sell them, and you may share whatever profit your work yields."

"I think we should take all the profits and buy more fabric," said one of the younger women, whose two children lived in the country with her widowed mother. Missing them, she was more ambitious than the others. "We could become dressmakers in our own right."

Olivia smiled. "You already are, Mrs. Tatman."

"Ladies, ladies, we must think this through very carefully," said Mr. Mullins. "Each of you has certain things you want to achieve for yourselves or your families. This could indeed be the beginning of a whole new enterprise, but we must think it through."

"I know you will make wise decisions, Mr. Mullins. Indeed, I have confidence in all of you. Now, I will leave you to it. Harold and I have other stops to make."

Practically coming to attention, the former soldier said, "Of course, and thank you, my lady. We will not disappoint you."

"I never dreamed that you would, Mr. Mullins." Turning and including all of them in her smile, she said, "Not any of you."

Olivia and Harold left the room. After stopping by the dying Mrs. Arvin's room, they returned to the carriage and set forth for the school. Harold squirmed with excitement in his seat.

Glancing out the window, he suddenly twitched all the curtains closed.

Frowning, his mistress asked, "What are you doing, Harold?"

"There's bodies out there a lady oughtn' see."

"Bodies?" she said, leaning over and peeking outside.

The carriage continued through another rather seedy part of the City. On the corner she spotted the bodies Harold was trying to hide. Two scantily clad females were talking to a red-nosed young man, their hands stroking his chest.

Dropping the curtain, Olivia said firmly, "I have seen that sort of female before, Harold. I am not likely to be shocked by such a spectacle."

Sitting back once more, her smooth brow was marred by a slight frown. After several minutes, she said, "I have to wonder what might happen if those women had the same opportunities. . . ."

"No, my lady. You cannot mean . . ."

"Well, it is hardly their fault, is it? I mean, they were innocents once, weren't they?"

"I doubt it," he grumbled.

"Still, I do see that it would be quite a challenge. I have helped one or two in the past, but it would be impossible to reach enough of them to make any real difference in the face of the City."

"That's right, my lady," said the servant, relaxing against the squabs again. He pulled out his book.

"I cannot help but speculate, though. Surely, there has to be someplace they gather, some central spot where I might . . ."

In response to her servant's sigh, Olivia grinned and relaxed against the soft velvet cushions.

The big man relaxed again, biting at his lip as he worked on deciphering the next word. He would not have been nearly as complacent had he seen the familiar gleam of determination in his mistress's eyes.

Their next stop took them to the edge of the City where the carriage pulled up before a neat brick building surrounded by an iron fence. Their arrival was heralded by a boy of about ten who flew down the steps to greet them at the gate.

"They're here!" he shouted over his shoulder, bobbing up and down like a bouncing ball. "They're here!"

With ponderous steps, the caretaker ambled up to the gate and turned his key in the lock. He stood to one side to allow them to enter.

"Good morning, Mr. Tucker," said Lady Olivia. "I trust you are well."

Another retired soldier, the man gave her a warm smile and nodded respectfully. "Thank ye, m'lady," he said, his voice a whisper.

Olivia masked the pity in her eyes and smiled brightly. Wounded on the Peninsula, the man had survived a saber wound to his throat, but his voice had never been the same.

Holding out her hand to the boy, Olivia said, "Good morning, Bobby." He wiped his hand on his breeches and took her gloved hand, bowing from the waist. "Oh, very well done. I can tell you have been practicing your manners."

"I practice with Mrs. Priddy and Mrs. Server every day, my lady." With an impish grin, he bowed again, though not as low this time. "Good morning, Mr. Harold."

"Good morning, young Bobby." Harold shook hands with the boy, and they followed Lady Olivia into the building.

The interior here was much like that of the widows' home. There was light everywhere. A row of more than twenty stair-stepped children lined the hall. Dressed neatly, they awaited Olivia's inspection. As before, she spoke to each child by name, tousling hair and shaking hands, and in the case of one small toddler, taking her up in her arms.

"And you, my bright Penny. How are you today?"

"Fine," came the grave reply.

With a final squeeze, she set the child down again and turned her attention to the headmistress who was dressed in dove gray, a soft color that belied her iron will.

"Good morning, Mrs. Priddy."

The woman curtsied and so did her subordinates.

"Good morning, my lady."

"I thought we could talk in your office while Harold gives his lesson to the little ones."

"Certainly. Mrs. Server, why don't you and Mr. Harold take the children to the schoolroom?"

"Yes, ma'am," said the younger version of the headmistress, though her regard was less severe.

When the headmistress and Olivia were alone with a teapot between them, Mrs. Priddy relaxed and smiled. "How are you, my dear Lady Olivia?"

"I am fine, Sarah. And you?"

"Wonderful, just wonderful. You know, every morning, when I open my eyes and see where I am, I . . . I cannot believe my good fortune—and it is all due to you, my dear."

"You are too kind, Sarah. I only provided the funds. This school is what you have made of it. I feel quite privileged to be a part of it."

"Now you are being kind," said the older woman, but there was pride in the lift of her chin as she glanced around the neat sitting room. "I may not have my Earnest, but I have my children, all twenty-two of them. I cannot be as lenient as a mother might be, but I believe they are happy here—even that little scapegrace, Bobby."

"Oh, he seems to have adjusted very well." They laughed. "The first time I saw him, I was doubtful of ever being able to get all the soot off of his skin. And his mouth!"

They shared a private laugh, and then Mrs. Priddy said, "I do hope your Mr. Harold is being careful of his vocabulary. I did worry about the letter, you know."

Olivia sipped her tea and said, "No need. He said he would use the word *fight*, but he would not demonstrate it with any great gestures."

"Good, good. The last time, it took me a week to keep the boys from pretend-fighting, and they were not nearly as meek as your Harold." Setting down her cup and saucer, the headmistress said, "When I think about it, I find it difficult to see how Mr. Harold ever succeeded at prizefighting. His is such a gentle soul."

"I think that is why he was not so very successful. Had he been more brutish, he might have won more bouts and been better able to fend off those debilitating injuries."

"But he is over his dizziness, you said."

"Oh yes," said Olivia. "Completely."

She wanted to pat the woman's hand, but this might make Sarah close her heart again. For some time, Olivia had suspected that her friend, one of her own former teachers, was developing warmer feelings for the gentle giant, but it would never do to reveal her suspicions. Sarah Priddy had survived heartrending tragedies in her short life—losing her soldier-husband and her two children within a month. When Olivia had found her again, Sarah had been unsociable and aloof. It would take a miracle to allow her to love again.

Instead, Olivia said brightly, "I have news for you. A friend of mine has agreed to allow Martin and Winnie to become apprentices at his country estate."

"How wonderful. Martin in the stables and Winnie in the kitchen?" Olivia nodded, and the headmistress said, "They will be thrilled. Never have a brother and sister fought so hard to stay together. This will finally allow them to do that and still be making their way in the world. I have worried so."

"I know. They are our little school's first success story. Why don't you go and tell them? I'll go to the schoolroom." They rose and walked to the door.

"Oh, that is where we will find all of them. None of them want to miss Harold's, uh, Mr. Harold's alphabet lesson."

In the schoolroom, it was just as she had said. The youngest children sat on the floor in a semicircle, their heads thrown back to look up at the big man. The other children had pulled up chairs or were standing close by, all watching and listening.

"Th' letter f is a strong little letter. It goes like this," he said, drawing the letter on a slate and holding it up for all to see. "It looks sort of like an old man who should have a cane but doesn't. See?" With this, he added eyes and a nose to the end of the hook. "Here's his face. These are his arms, and this . . . this is his humped-up back because he's so old, you know."

With a bit of a sneer, one young man of twelve

said, "I seen a fellow like that once. 'E was pullin' a cart o' vegetables like a donkey."

Mrs. Priddy took a step toward this young man, but before she could speak, Harold said, "I reckon that man was just like this one—working hard for his family—another word that starts wif' an *f*. You know, family, like all o' you here is."

"We're not a family, Mr. Harold," said Bobby. "We don't have a mum or a dad."

"Not exactly, but you have Mrs. Priddy and the other ladies to be your mums."

"But no pa," said the first boy, his sneer fading into a pout.

"Not a pa, but you've got me. I'm like an uncle who comes t' visit every day or two. An' you've got Mr. Tucker, a real war hero, he is."

"But he can't talk right."

"Can you understand him?" The children nodded. "Can you hear him, even though you have to get close?" They nodded again. "Then there's another uncle for you. And you've got plenty o' brothers and sisters t' fight with. See? You're a real family, and if anybody says you're not, they'll have t' answer t' me."

"Will you fight them?" asked Bobby eagerly.

Harold looked at Mrs. Priddy and grinned. Shaking his head, he said, "No, but I'll tell them what's what, I will. And who would argue with me? Now, tell me again, what words begin with this little letter?" He held up his drawing again, and the children began to call out words.

Their visit to the school complete, the coachman turned the carriage toward Bond Street to the millinery shop. There, Olivia selected several lengths of colorful ribbon to trim her old bonnet. This task accomplished, she purchased an ostrich plume, dyed a lovely willow green, for her aunt's favorite turban.

As she left the shop, she collided with the tall, scowling Lord Sheridan. Offering a gruff apology, he leaned over to retrieve her small packet of ribbons and his cane.

Straightening again, the ostrich plume she held slapped his face, and he shoved it away roughly. It fluttered to the ground, and he bent to retrieve this, too.

Thrusting it into her hand, he grumbled, "Demmed feather."

"No, my lord," she replied sweetly.

Squinting at her through the green tendrils, he pushed them aside and peered down at her. With a swift motion, his quizzing glass went up and so did his nose.

"I beg your pardon."

"I said it is neither demmed nor is it a feather. It is a plume, an ostrich plume, to be correct."

Olivia took a step back as the scent of spirits assaulted her nose. She gave him her best smile and prepared to move along. No sense in trying to converse with a man in his cups.

His hand on her shoulder prevented her progress. Harold, watching from his station by the carriage door, took a step toward them. Olivia shook her head.

"Are you making game of me, Miss . . ."

"Lady Olivia Cunningham, Lord Sheridan. We may not have been formally introduced but we have met, and quite recently, too. Surely you remember last night?"

Still staring at her through that awful magnifying glass, he cleared his throat. "Beg pardon, Lady Olivia. Here is your package. Good day."

With this, he was gone. Olivia shook her head and watched him walk away. His gait was steady and sure. Had he not been forced to lean over—twice—she was certain no one would have been able to detect his drunken state. With a shrug of her slim shoulders, she walked to the carriage.

Olivia climbed inside, and Harold joined her. He signaled the coachman to start. In the distance, church bells chimed the hour.

Four o'clock. Olivia sighed.

Lord Sheridan in his cups so early in the day. What a waste of such a fine figure of a man. He must be terribly unhappy.

"Dash it, Fenwick! I can do it myself!"

"Certainly, m'lord," said the valet, continuing to brush his master's waistcoat while Lord Sheridan tore off his ruined cravat and began once again.

"Hell and blast!"

The valet presented yet another cravat. Drew eyed it with suspicion and then muttered, "Oh, tie the blasted thing yourself. I'm all thumbs tonight!"

"Very good, m'lord." Moments later, the valet stepped away to allow his master a view of the masterfully styled cravat.

"Yes, well, that is quite acceptable." Drew glanced at the valet's stricken face and added, "More than acceptable, of course. You have outdone yourself yet again, Fenwick. Thank you."

"You are very welcome, m'lord. We are wearing the black coat this evening, are we not?"

"Indeed we are. The color suits my mood perfectly."

"I hope your indisposition is not the result of any inefficiency on my part or that of any member of your staff, m'lord."

"Of course it isn't, as you well know. It is the result of a man going to his club too early and imbibing far too much good port with a friend who has a head made of iron. I do not, unfortunately. Now, I must meet with my same friend for a demmed rout, of all things, but I shall come about."

"Of course, m'lord."

Drew shrugged into the coat. "There is one thing, Fenwick." The valet continued to fuss over his coat. "I didn't bring home a woman this afternoon, did I?"

"A woman? To this house?"

"A lady, perhaps?"

"Oh no, m'lord. You have not done such a thing since you were a youth. How well I remember the expression on the dowager countess's face!"

"Yes, well, that is a relief. Yes, I will do nicely. Do not wait up for me, Fenwick. I can put myself to bed."

"Very good, m'lord."

Drew smiled as he strolled out the door to the stairs. Every night it was the same. He told Fenwick he could put himself to bed. Fenwick agreed and then waited up anyway. It was the result of too many years of dedicated service.

"Sir Richard is in the drawing room, m'lord," said the butler when Drew reached the hall below.

"Thank you, Silvers."

His hand on the door, Drew paused. He could have sworn he had spent some time with a woman that afternoon. A blurry cloud of blond hair and china-blue eyes kept presenting itself in his aching head. Rubbish, of course. He had not visited the brothels since his youth, either, and he did not have a mistress at the moment.

Pasting a smile on his face, he opened the door.

"Ready for an evening of madcap frivolity, old boy?" asked the dapper Sir Richard.

"Ready as I will ever be."

"Where is your cane?"

"Silvers has it in the hall."

"Which is it tonight?"

"The silver wolf with the ruby eyes."

"Perfect," said Sir Richard, clapping Drew on the shoulder. At Drew's raised brow, he added, "It will match your bloodshot eyes to perfection!"

"Devil a bit!" replied Drew. As they left the room, he asked, "Are we picking up Maddie on the way?"

"Heavens no! You know her thoughts on attending a rout." Raising his voice, he mimicked, "A more colossal waste of time you will never find— not to mention the discomfort of squeezing up and down a narrow staircase with a hundred other fools, most of whom have never made use of soap and have instead bathed in the most foul-smelling cologne ever made."

"Succinct enough. You have Maddie down very

well," said Drew, entering the carriage. "Perhaps we have all been spending too much time together this Season."

"Never say you are tiring of our company. I may be forced to re-enlist," said Sir Richard.

"Not at all. I am enjoying this Season very much more than the last two without you. Maddie is all well and good, but she cannot accompany me to Manton's for shooting or Jackson's Boxing Salon."

"Nor can she join us at White's—a pity, I say. Perhaps you and I should begin a new club in which ladies are allowed."

"My, yes, wouldn't that be well attended?" drawled Drew. "Besides, there is no need for another such club. You can always go to Watier's with a friend."

"Not all the time and not the same caliber of female as our Maddie," said Sir Richard.

"Certainly not."

"Have you wondered why she never remarried after old Thorpe snuffed it?" asked his friend.

"I asked her once," said Drew, and Richard cocked his head to one side in surprise. "We were at a musicale or some such entertainment and were trying to converse so as to drown out the screechings of some young miss demonstrating her singular lack of talent on the harp."

"Ah, and how did our Maddie reply?"

"Only that since Thorpe left her very well set for life, she didn't feel any particular need to ever be mauled about again. I didn't wish to pursue the topic further."

The two men exchanged understanding glances and looked out the windows, lost in their own thoughts. Drew, who knew that Richard had once been enamored of their friend Maddie, wondered how he was digesting this bit of information. Could there still be some feelings there? Probably not. They had been in their salad days, all of them, a time when love had flamed at the mere batting of a girl's eyelashes.

The carriage came to a stop, and a footman threw open the door. Drew hopped to the ground first.

Facing the house, ablaze with candles, he said, "Have you buttoned up your coat, Richard? I once attended one of these routs and forgot to fasten my coat. As I was going up the stairs, I turned the wrong way, and suddenly another fellow, coming down the stairs, found himself wearing my coat. I never did get it back."

Laughing, the two elegant gentlemen entered the house, squeezed into the hall and began the trek up the stairs to greet their host and hostess, Lord and Lady Stone.

The Marquess of Sheridan had his quizzing glass in one hand, ready to depress the attention of any mushrooms, and his silver-handled cane in the other. It was warm, too warm, and sweat trickled between his shoulder blades.

"Should have come earlier," he muttered over his shoulder.

Sir Richard said, "Wouldn't have done any good. Even if we had been the very first guests, it would have been devilish unpleasant getting back down the stairs. The other drawback, of course, is that we actually might have been forced into polite conversation with our hostess."

Drew chuckled at this, nodding in agreement. He then turned his attention to putting one foot in front of the other while trying to avoid the press of other elegantly dressed guests. Glancing up the stairs, the candles in the sconces on the wall dazzled his eyes. It was then that he saw her, the vision from his afternoon daze. A blue gown, shimmering in the candlelight, covering a form that was round in all the right places. The curls bobbing up and down were golden, and the eyes—a celestial . . .

"Hell and blast!" he exclaimed, dropping the quizzing glass as the vision of loveliness took on an identity.

Beside him, a matron in a hideous purple turban gasped in feigned shock at his language.

"What is it?" asked his friend, placing a hand on Drew's shoulder.

"It's that dashed silly gudgeon from last night!"

"I . . . I am going to swoon," whined a high-pitched voice just in front of them. The herd of people kept moving.

"Make some room! Give her some air!" ordered the vision of loveliness. "Miss Featherstone, take my hand. Oh, my dear girl . . . I . . ."

The insensible girl slumped against Lady Olivia. Her blue eyes pleaded for help. With a growl, Drew gathered the unconscious Miss Featherstone into his arms, threw her over his shoulder, and turned.

"Make way! Make way!" he commanded. As if by magic, a pathway opened, and he quickly carried the limp figure down the stairs to the hall, not stopping until he had found an empty room—the library, by the look of it. With a grunt, he deposited the girl on the nearest sofa.

"Oh, thank you, Lord Sheridan! It is most kind of you!" said Lady Olivia, who had followed him into the room. She hovered over the girl, wringing her hands.

Drew scowled at both of them but didn't speak.

Sir Richard strolled into the library, granted the prostrate girl an amused glance, and said, "How do you do, my lady? Sir Richard Adair, at your service."

That dazzling smile turned to face his friend. Drew expelled a growl and said, "Do you have any smelling salts, my lady?"

"I believe Miss Featherstone carries some with her . . . in . . . her reticule." She was shocked when Drew plucked Miss Featherstone's reticule from her wrist. "You should not be doing that, my lord. I will . . . I must protest. It is most improper for a gentleman to open a lady's reticule."

Ignoring her, he opened it and fished through the contents until he felt a small vial. Lady Olivia expelled a gasp of irritation and snatched the bottle from his hands. She waved it in the vicinity of Miss Featherstone's nose. The girl wheezed, lifted her head, and then fell back against the leather couch. The door opened, and a mature lady dressed in wisps of gray floated into the room.

"What in the world are you doing in here, Olivia? I lost you. If a footman had not noticed where you had gone, I . . . Oh, gentlemen. Good evening. I don't believe we have had the pleasure. I am Miss Hepplewhite, Lady Olivia's aunt."

Sir Richard executed an elegant bow over Miss Hepplewhite's hand, but Drew merely nodded.

"Miss Featherstone swooned as I was passing her on the stairs," said Lady Olivia. She added flatly, "Lord Sheridan carried her in here."

His dark eyes sparked with amusement. "And then I made your, uh . . . niece, is it?" At the older woman's nod of confirmation, he continued, "I made your niece angry by going through the silly chit's reticule for her smelling salts."

"I don't doubt it. Olivia, when did you start carrying smelling salts? You never swoon."

"Of course I do not," she said, pursing her lips.

"No, it was Miss Featherstone's reticule I invaded," he added, a smile playing on his lips. "And now, Lady Olivia is unreservedly cross with me."

She met the challenge in his eyes with a flash of spirit, quickly extinguished as he waited. The vapid smile reappeared.

"I am not in the least cross with you, Lord Sheridan. How could I be? You saved the day, and I am certain Miss Featherstone will thank you when she revives sufficiently."

In the face of this nauseating optimism, the shutters closed over his eyes, and he said derisively, "Drivel. I only did what was necessary. Good evening, ladies. Richard, shall we go?"

He didn't wait for his friend's reply but strode out the door, down the narrow corridor, and outside. On the pavement, he paced for a moment, ignoring the greetings of the other guests who were getting down from their carriages. With a snort,

Drew continued down the street, his cane tucked under his arm and his pace decisive.

Tearing off her crown of blue silk roses, Olivia declared, "Of all the maddening men I have met, Lord Sheridan is the most maddening!"

Her aunt sat down on the sofa in their neat drawing room and said sensibly, "I cannot understand why you would say such a thing, Olivia. He was merely demurring at your praise."

"Demurring, my foot! He was insulting! And the way he looked down his nose at me was insulting, too!"

"I think you are exaggerating, my dear. He was looking down because you were sitting next to Miss Featherstone, and the marquess is, after all, so deliciously tall."

"Rubbish," she said, pursing her lips.

"Do sit down, my dear. There is no need to get into such a state. Let me order the tea tray. The staff will be surprised that we are home so early, but I am certain Cook will be able to put something together for us. She spent the entire day baking, you know."

"You go ahead, Aunt. I could not swallow a morsel."

Olivia paced the length of the room. When she returned and sat down on the sofa beside her aunt, she smiled. "Forgive me for my display of temper. I really do not know what came over me. I am not usually so cross."

"No, you are not. Ah, here is Witchell with the tea tray already. You read my mind, Witchell."

Aunt Amy busied herself with the tray, pouring two cups of tea, putting a spoonful of sugar in one and three in the other. She handed the first to Olivia and then took a deep drink of the other.

"Ah, that is good. And let's see what Cook has for us this evening. Macaroons, my favorite. Oh, and a little strawberry tart for you, my dear?"

Deep in thought, Olivia did not reply. Her aunt put one of the tarts on a plate and placed it on her niece's lap.

"Oh, thank you, Aunt." She took a bite and then replaced it on the plate. "Quite good. I must tell Cook she has outdone herself."

A moment passed in silence. Aunt Amy glanced at the forgotten tart and clucked her tongue.

"Such a waste. And you know the best praise a cook can receive is to have her offerings eaten."

Olivia then looked at the tart and smiled. Dutifully, she popped the rest of it into her mouth.

"That is much better. Now, perhaps we should discuss this problem you are having with the marquess. Such a handsome man! Oh, his friend, too. And so charming. Sir Richard, I mean. To remain with us until Miss Featherstone regained her senses and then to accompany us home. It was quite gallant of him."

"Yes, he seems a nice enough gentleman, despite the company he keeps."

"Dear, dear, you do have a grudge against the marquess. Whatever has he done to deserve that? It is not like you."

"No, it is not."

With a coy grin, her aunt said, "Have you perhaps formed a secret tendre for the handsome Lord Sheridan?"

"A tendre?" said Olivia, placing her cup on the tray and rising. "I cannot bear the man, he is . . ."

"But I didn't even know you had met the man!" exclaimed her aunt. "It is very puzzling. You, who likes everyone, taking this handsome man in dislike. I mean, he did bump into you at the Pinchot's ball, but that is hardly a reason to inspire such disgust. Besides, he sent you flowers today along with a lovely note of apology."

"The flowers were well enough, but I wager his secretary wrote the note. I cannot imagine that one such as Lord Sheridan would ever admit to being clumsy. He also said he was sorry, and such a kind sentiment is hardly likely to spring forth from one such as he."

"Olivia! How uncharitable of you to say such a thing."

Olivia nibbled her lower lip, looking very like a naughty child. Finally, scuffling her feet, she said, "I am sorry, Aunt. I don't know why I have taken the man in dislike, but I have. I had even wondered about helping him to find someone, someone who could make him smile. He is always so glum, you know. But now, I can see little sense in it. He would probably bite the hand that fed him."

"What?"

Olivia frowned and said, "Oh, you know what I mean." She sighed. "I am going to bed. Perhaps in the morning my usual sunny self will reappear." Leaning down, she kissed her aunt's cheek before strolling out of the room.

* * *

In her room, Olivia was silent as her sniffling maid helped her change into her nightdress. Bidding the servant a weak good night, she climbed into bed.

The fact that her abigail was still ill suddenly hit her, and she started to rise. Then she subsided. She was in no mood to chat with Pansy about her illness.

A moment later, a gray fluff of fur jumped onto the foot of the bed and then sauntered up to the head to be petted.

"Oh, Hawkeye, what am I to do? Why does that man make me want to strangle him?" She scratched under the cat's chin and said, "Yes, yes, I know I should not blame him for running into me outside the millinery shop today. It was more of a mere bumping into than running into, and I'm sure he did not plan to get foxed and then accost me."

"Meow."

"Exactly. It is not so much what he does or says, it is the manner in which it is delivered. Really, I don't expect every male who sees me to fall helplessly in love with me. You might have, but then, you are very easily won over, aren't you?"

The cat's purring distracted her, and she scratched him behind his ear. When she stopped, he looked at her with his one eye, blinked, and then hopped off the bed.

Olivia blew out the candle and pulled up the covers. Though it was late April, the evenings were still quite brisk. The small fire on the other side of the room did little to ward off the chill. She shivered and closed her eyes.

Not for the first time she wondered what it

would be like to snuggle close to someone for warmth, for strength. The image of the infuriating Lord Sheridan taunted her. With a twitch of the covers, she turned on her side and forced herself to think of spring flowers, little puppies, and children's laughter.

She refused to allow such an aggravating man to spoil her rest!

CHAPTER THREE

As Olivia had hoped, morning brought with it her usually sunny self. She rose and went to the window that overlooked the narrow garden and smiled. How could she be anything but happy on such a sunny day? Below, the gardener's boy was throwing the stick for Hasty, who chased it with great speed, despite his lack of one leg. The big mutt returned the stick and dropped it on the ground before licking the boy's face. As always, Olivia's heart ached to think of the poor, mistreated animal she had rescued from the gutters in Cheapside.

She turned away and rang for her maid. When the door opened, she frowned and said, "What is it, Jinks? Where is Pansy?"

"She is still in her bed, m'lady. I fear that cough of hers is getting worse. And she's got a fever, too."

"I must go to her at once." Olivia threw on a wrapper and hurried down the hall and up the back stairs to the servant's quarters. Her maid was covered up to her chin in several blankets and was still shivering. Olivia sat on the edge of the narrow cot and put her hand on her maid's burning forehead.

"My goodness, Pansy. You should have sent for me. Jinks, get one of the footmen up here immediately to light a fire. Then tell Witchell to send for the physician."

"Yes, m'lady." The other maid hurried away.

Olivia looked at the water on the bedside table and poured a glass for the shivering maid. "Drink this. You must have lots to drink if you are to fight this fever."

The maid obeyed but then fell back against the pillow and said, "Please go, m'lady. I don't want you to get sick."

"I am never ill, as you well know. And someone must look after you. Now, close your eyes and sleep."

Olivia went down to dress. When she returned, she remained by the maid's side until the doctor arrived. After examining the maid, he motioned to Olivia to join him in the corridor.

"She is very ill, Lady Olivia. It will be touch and go. She seems a healthy girl. If she will do as she is told, I think she will recover. Have someone sit with her the rest of today and tonight—someone who is fit and unlikely to contract the disease."

"What do you think it is?"

"Pneumonia, I fear, or as near to pneumonia as one can get. I have given her laudanum to help her rest. Give her enough to help her sleep through the day and night. I will come back tomorrow morning and see how she does."

"Thank you for coming so quickly, Doctor."

The sober man gave her a rusty smile and said, "When the footman said to come quickly, I feared it might be your formidable aunt."

"Hardly. She is as healthy as a horse."

"An admirable woman, your aunt."

"I shall tell her you said so."

"No need. She knows what I think of her already. It never made any difference." With this cryptic remark, he gave a nod and hurried away.

Olivia returned to her maid's side to watch her sleep. While there, she puzzled over Mr. Jenson's comment about her aunt. The physician was from Wiltshire and had grown up near the same village as her mother and aunt. He had known her aunt forever, but his words indicated that there was more to their story than her aunt had ever revealed.

Perhaps the good doctor had been an unsuccessful suitor for her aunt's hand. Olivia had often wondered about her aunt's past. There had never been any talk of thwarted love, but there had never been an uncle either. She resolved to ask her aunt about the good doctor at the first opportunity.

Olivia left Pansy only long enough to fetch the novel she was currently reading. There she sat for the rest of the day, quite content to read and serve the servant her broth when she awoke briefly. With the evening dose of laudanum, one of the other chambermaids named Missy entered the sickroom.

She dropped a quick curtsey to Olivia's greeting.

"If it pleases you, m'lady, I'm here to sit with our

Pansy through the night." She pointed to the second cot and added, "That's my cot right there, but I won't sleep. I'll keep watch, I promise."

"I'm sure you will, Missy. I have given her the medicine the doctor left. She seems to be resting quietly now, and I think her fever has come down. You must send to the kitchen for broth if she wakes in the middle of the night."

"Very good, m'lady."

"I am going out, but Mr. Witchell will know how to find me, should I be needed."

"She does look much better, m'lady. I'm sure she will be fine."

"Let us hope so. I consider all of you indispensable to this household, you know. Good night."

"Good night, m'lady."

In the hall, Olivia stretched her weary muscles and trudged downstairs to her own room. There, a footman was just leaving, having brought a tray laden with all sorts of tempting fare.

With layers of wrapper and shifts streaming behind her, Olivia's aunt sailed into the room, inspected the tray, and said, "Sit down at once, my dear. You must be exhausted and famished. How is Pansy?"

Olivia shook her head, but she sat down at the table and filled a plate. "Better, I think, but only time will tell. By the way, did you see Mr. Jenson today?"

"No, why should I see that man? I am not ill, and if I were, I would not send for him."

"Really? I thought the two of you were friends."

"At one time, perhaps, but no more."

"Then I am surprised to hear you speak of him with such vehemence. I mean, if he means nothing to you, why should you . . ."

"Ah, I see what you are about, sly puss. You mean to insinuate that there was some episode that caused us to have a rift. Not at all. I barely remember the man. As for knowing him as a boy, he was nothing but a grubby, little thing. I used to follow him and my brother everywhere, but that was when I was only a child. No, there is nothing that happened between us."

"If you say so," replied Olivia, hiding her skeptical smile behind her serviette.

"And so I do. You know how I feel about doctors. For the most part, they do more harm than good, and Mr. Jenson is no exception. Except, perhaps, that he has the most atrocious manners."

"Very well then. We will not speak of him again. Won't you join me?"

"No, I have already eaten a little something. Why don't we stay at home tonight, my dear? You must be exhausted."

"I am tired, but I cannot miss the Grants' ball. According to Lady Grant, that old miser Pendleton is supposed to attend. I have been trying for months to have a word with him over that new school I want to build in Richmond. He so rarely attends anything since his young wife died two years ago."

"Such a shame. Both her and the babe. Who would have thought she would go before him?"

"Yes, a tragedy, but he might as well find some charities to give some of that money to as he doesn't have a direct heir, and I want that school to be one of them."

"But he won't part with a single groat while he is alive."

"I think I will be able to persuade him."

"If anyone can, it is you, my dear. Very well, then eat up. I will have Jinks come in to help you dress when she is done with me." At the door, her aunt said, "I am glad to see that your mood has improved."

Olivia grinned and said, "Was there ever any doubt?"

She finished her meal and began to strip off the round gown she wore. Looking at herself in the mirror, she gave a sigh of satisfaction. She was only five and twenty, but she could still pass as a miss in her first Season. Not that she was worried about pleasing the gentlemen. Even if she never married, she had her good works to keep her busy and happy.

On the wall behind the cheval glass, her mother's small portrait smiled at her. Her mother had been quite a philanthropist in her own right. She had come from wealthy stock and had left Olivia a small fortune. The rest of Olivia's vast fortune had come from her father, the Earl of Carstairs, whom she barely remembered.

When Olivia had been younger and seriously looking for a husband, her aunt's words of caution had constantly rung in her ears. She had been careful not to become attached to a fortune hunter, but now, at five and twenty, she had no one, and she had become accustomed to her unmarried state. What was more, the gentlemen had come to accept it, too. Last Season, she had received only two offers of marriage—both acceptable, but both rejected. She had decided to settle for nothing less than love, and if that meant spending her life unwed, then so be it.

Her aunt's maid entered the room and pulled the emerald-green silk gown from the wardrobe. Olivia stepped into it and stood patiently as the servant expertly pinned and taped it into place.

"Will you be wearing the Cunningham emeralds or the single pendant, my lady?"

"I think the Cunningham emeralds are in order if I am to impress Mr. Pendleton tonight. And the matching tiara, too."

"Very good, my lady."

Finally, the maid pronounced her masterpiece complete and stepped back to allow Olivia a look at her blond hair. It was piled on top of her head, lending her height. On top of the cluster of curls was the emerald-and-diamond tiara, winking at her in the candlelight.

"You have outdone yourself, Jinks."

"Thank you, my lady."

"Would you mind running upstairs and checking on Pansy for me? I hate to leave without first inquiring about her progress."

"Very good, my lady."

A moment later, the maid returned and informed Olivia that her abigail was sleeping peacefully. Olivia made her way down the stairs to the drawing room where her aunt waited for her, talking quietly with Olivia's friend Lord Hardcastle. He rose and bowed when she entered the room. Olivia found the look of admiration on his face very gratifying, especially because he was in love with the simpering Miss Featherstone.

"I am a lucky fellow, escorting two such beautiful creatures to the ball this evening. Your aunt has just been telling me about your maid. I do hope she makes a full recovery."

"I am hopeful, too, but tomorrow will tell, I think. Meanwhile, one of the other maids has promised to keep vigil tonight and to send for me if there is a need."

"If I had to live my life as a servant, Olivia, I think I would not mind being one of yours. You treat them much better than the average employer," said Tony.

Olivia said, "But I am not just their employer. We are not friends, precisely, but they know they can depend on me just as I depend on them. My mother taught me to always remember the Golden Rule when it came to my servants."

"A wise woman, your mother," said her aunt. "Now, shall we go? I do not want to miss out on a minute of the card room activities. The Grants always have the best card rooms for their balls. I think Lord Grant would operate his own club if his wife would countenance such a scheme."

"I understand he did operate such a place for a short time," said Tony.

"A gambling hell?" said Aunt Amy with a delicious shiver.

"Not a hell, but a very lively place. I visited it once and nearly lost my entire inheritance."

"Oh, Tony, now you are teasing Aunt Amy, and it is very bad of you."

He crossed his heart and said, "'Struth, Miss Hepplewhite. 'Pon my honor."

Olivia laughed and said, "Now I know he is making up tales. He always speaks in one-syllable words when he is attempting to pull the wool over your eyes."

"I must protest!" he exclaimed, ushering them out the front door.

Their short journey to the Grants' town house was filled with lively conversation. Olivia laughed until her sides hurt, and she was gasping for air by the time they pulled up to the house.

Inside, they greeted their host and hostess and then entered the large ballroom. The colorful gowns swirled, contrasting perfectly with the gentlemen's dark coats. Jewels twinkled in the candlelight as if keeping time with the musicians' instruments.

Olivia smiled, her blue eyes dancing in delight. It was a perfect picture of the elite of English Society, and, as always, she was thrilled to be a part of it.

Tony excused himself, and Olivia's aunt leaned close and whispered, "Exactly why is it you rejected Lord Hardcastle's suit? He is one of the most handsome and charming men in all of London. If I were twenty years younger . . ."

"He is all that and more, but he is one of my oldest friends—more like a brother than a suitor—and you would have me wed him? I think not."

Aunt Amy sighed. "I suppose not, but time is passing, my dear girl. I cannot help but wonder, when?"

"When I am ready. Or never. At the moment, there is no one who could make me want to change the current state of my life. Now, we are here to enjoy ourselves. There is Lady Fairfax, craning her neck to gain your attention. You must join her before she falls out of her chair," said Olivia with a giggle.

"Wretched child," replied her aunt.

"Wretched, indeed!" exclaimed a dapper gentleman, coming to beg a dance. "Your aunt's eyesight must be failing. There is nothing wretched about you this evening."

"Just the fond rambling of a dear relative. How are you, Mr. Thomas? And your mother? I was sorry to hear she was ailing again."

"She is much improved. As for me, I am splendid now that I have found you before the rest of your admirers. Would you do me the honor of the next dance?"

"With pleasure."

"Wonderful. We can chat until it is time. Oh, look, there is my cousin, Sir Richard. Have you had the chance to meet him? He has only recently sold out his commission in the army and returned to us. A capital fellow. Quite the hero, he is."

"We haven't been formally introduced, but I have had the pleasure of his company," said Olivia. A little shiver ran up her spine as they approached the usually unapproachable cluster of elegants.

"Good evening, Cousin. Lady Olivia, may I present my cousin, Sir Richard Adair? Richard, this is Lady Olivia Cunningham."

Sir Richard made a leg and said, "Lady Olivia and I have met, after a fashion. I hope you and your aunt are none the worse for Miss Featherstone's unfortunate incident last night."

"We are fine, and so is Miss Featherstone, thank you. You were most helpful." She could not prevent herself from emphasizing the word *you* while glancing at his handsome friend, the debonair Lord Sheridan.

The marquess actually smiled, and Olivia felt the blood rush to her face. He had understood her sarcasm perfectly.

"I did very little, really," protested Sir Richard. "Your Miss Featherstone is very lucky to have such steadfast friends as you and your charming aunt."

"But Miss Featherstone is a charming young lady," replied Olivia, ignoring the warmth in his eyes.

"But I am being rude," said Mr. Thomas. "I should introduce you to Sheri here. This is Lord Sheridan, perhaps you have met."

At the same instant, Olivia and Lord Sheridan said, "We have."

Olivia, realizing her tone had been less than cordial, smiled at the marquess and added, "That is, we have run into each other a time or two."

"Oh, yes, at the ball a few nights ago. Quite so," said Sir Richard.

"Quite so," replied the marquess, his gaze somewhere over the top of Olivia's head.

Olivia wanted to stamp her foot, but she fixed her smile on her face and glanced back at the dance floor, remarking, "Isn't this a pretty setting for a ball."

"Very pretty," said Mr. Thomas.

"Candlelight, paint, a floor. A typical ballroom, surely," said Lord Sheridan, his dark eyes challenging hers.

"But quite spacious, and the music is . . ."

"Music," he added, fixing his gaze on hers.

She continued to smile and looked away. Not by so much as a heaving bosom did she let him know that he had nettled her.

"Ah, time for the next set. If you will excuse us?" said Mr. Thomas, offering Olivia his arm.

"Only if I may have the pleasure of the next dance with you, Lady Olivia," said Sir Richard.

"I would enjoy that immensely," she replied, taking Mr. Thomas's arm and walking away.

"What a perfect ninny," said the marquess, just loudly enough for her to hear.

Olivia ignored it and him. If he had taken her in dislike for some reason, there was nothing she could do about it. Besides, why should she wish to change the opinion of such an odious man?

Then she was in Mr. Thomas's arms, waltzing around the floor without a care in the world. When the music ended, she was glad to see Sir Richard approaching her, away from the piercing eyes of Lord Sheridan.

"What a wonderful night," he said, when the country dance brought them together.

"Then you must not be as cynical as your friend Lord Sheridan," said Olivia.

Bending close to her ear, he said, "No one is as cynical as my friend Sheri."

"What is it that makes him so . . ."

"Surly?"

They separated, and Olivia hoped that he would pick up their conversation where they had left off. She was not disappointed.

"Sheri can't help it. He has lost his rose-tinted spectacles."

She chuckled and asked, "Must one have rose-tinted spectacles to enjoy living?"

"Most definitely. Either that, or one must dance with a beautiful lady at least once every single day. Myself, now, I don't need those spectacles at all."

This was said with a speaking glance that made Olivia giggle.

When they next came together, he had put on a long face and moaned, "You doubt my words?"

"I think your words are delightful nonsense, and I am very entertained but not taken in, Sir Richard."

He clasped his hand to his breast and said, "You wound me, good lady." She made a face, and he added dramatically, "Never fear. I shall come about. I shall simply work harder to persuade you of my sincerity."

"A labor of impossibility," she said.

"A labor of love," he whispered with a wink.

She laughed, her heart light and cheery. Glancing about her, she saw the Marquess of Sheridan greeting his friend, Lady Madeline Thorpe. There was that flash of a smile again—the type of smile that could make a lady forget how maddening the man could be. She wondered if the widowed Lady Thorpe and Lord Sheridan were . . . Olivia swallowed the lump in her throat that this thought brought with it.

"They are only friends," said Sir Richard, claiming her hand once again and reading her mind perfectly.

"I . . . I don't know what you mean," she said.

"Sheri and Maddie grew up together. They are only friends."

Her nose in the air, she said, "I am certain it is no concern of mine. That is, I did wonder. Lord Sheridan is so very unhappy, I thought perhaps he and Lady Thorpe . . ."

"No hope for that. What about me? I grew up with them, too. Are you not worried that Lady Thorpe and I . . ."

"I assure you, Sir Richard, I have not thought of it at all, much less worried about it."

The music stopped, and she took his arm.

His expression woebegone, he heaved a sigh and said, "Just my luck."

"What is, sir?"

"That you have not given me any thought at all. Ah well, perhaps someday . . ."

"You are being absurd, Sir Richard."

"I do try, my lady. I really do try." He grinned and handed her to her next partner.

Olivia passed from one partner to the next, engaging in perfectly amenable conversation. This, she told herself, was what she was bred for, what she reveled in. The occasional glance at the disagreeable marquess did nothing to lower her spirits as she danced and laughed.

The supper dance was announced, and Olivia realized she had forgotten her original reason for attending the ball that evening—to persuade Mr. Pendleton to part with some of his money for the new school. She had watched him enter the ballroom and then detour to the card room, but that was the last she had seen of him.

Supper was announced, and she found herself on Lord Hardcastle's arm. Miss Featherstone had not felt up to attending, so Tony was very happy to escort his friend to supper.

"Have you seen Mr. Pendleton?" she whispered.

"Not at all. Wait a minute. Isn't that the old miser over there, coming out of the card room with your aunt on his arm?"

"So it is," said Olivia, giving a little wave to her aunt, who towed the wealthy old man toward them.

"Good evening, Mr. Pendleton," said Olivia. "Have you met Lord Hardcastle?"

"No, no reason to have met the boy, is there? How d'you do, my lord?"

"Very well, thank you, sir. Delighted to make your acquaintance."

They strolled into the dining hall and began to fill their plates at the buffet.

When they were finally seated, Mr. Pendleton said, "I see you have enlisted your aunt's help in this latest bid for my fortune, young lady."

"Bid for your fortune?" said Olivia, nearly choking on her asparagus.

"Do not play the simpleton with me, my girl. Your aunt did her best to do me out of my fortune in the card room. I finally had to make her my partner to prevent her from lining her pockets with my gold. And then she told me she wanted me to help build that orphanage for you."

"A school for orphans and other poor children. A place where they could become good citizens, sir, and contribute to the good of society."

"A pretty speech, but why should I care what becomes of a group of unruly urchins?" The toothy old man watched her like a cat playing with a mouse.

"I would be happy to show you why, sir. You are welcome to accompany me to the school where the children now live and learn. You will see what a difference it has made to all of them."

He cackled at this and shook his head. "Heaven forfend, Lady Olivia! I will give you the money you request, if only to prevent you from dragging me anywhere to witness your good works."

"Thank you, Mr. Pendleton. And should you change your mind and ever wish to see . . ." He shook his head decisively, and Olivia retreated with her victory intact. "Very well, then I will simply say thank you."

They were soon joined by several other couples, and the conversation became general. Olivia was having a delightful evening, and only occasionally thought of her sick maid at home or the dour Lord Sheridan.

When she chanced to look around, she could tell that he and his friends were also having a merry time. Their conversation seemed to consist of one person speaking in an undertone and the rest of their company erupting into laughter. The next time, another of their group would speak, and the same thing occurred.

To Olivia, their behavior bordered on the rude. She watched surreptitiously as their host, Lord Grant, strolled by and paused to chat with them. He was smiling as he walked away, and Olivia chided herself for being so judgmental.

Tapping her arm, Mr. Pendleton asked quietly,

"Why are you so interested in that group over there, Lady Olivia?"

"I am sorry, sir. I didn't mean to be rude."

"You weren't," he replied. Nodding toward Lord Sheridan's group, he said, "They call themselves the misanthropists, you know. They take their pleasure in disparaging others. They find Society lacking, but unlike you, they do nothing to remedy its ills."

"I . . . I had heard the term, but I wasn't quite certain why they were called that."

"Just a bunch of unhappy people, if you ask me. I may not be a jolly sort of chap, but I don't dislike my fellow man. I just prefer my own company most of the time."

Olivia turned her smile on him and said, "We are glad you chose to join us this evening, Mr. Pendleton."

"Because of my money?"

"No, because we, my aunt and I, like your company."

He sat back and fairly beamed at this. Olivia felt a twinge of shame. She did like Mr. Pendleton, but would she have liked him so well if he had been poor? What if he had turned down her request?

How hypocritical of her to vilify Lord Sheridan and his friends when she was no better. She must try to be more tolerant.

"Olivia, Mr. Pendleton has suggested a ride into the countryside tomorrow afternoon, to Richmond, if the weather holds fine," said her aunt.

"A marvelous idea! Shall we make it a picnic?"

"If that is what you ladies want, why not?" said

the old man, giving them all a view of his toothy smile. "Shall we say eleven o'clock? Or is that too early for you young people?"

"Not at all, sir," said Lord Hardcastle. "Might I bring Miss Featherstone? I have an, uh, appointment in the morning at her house."

"Ah, sits the wind in that corner? Then, of course, you must bring Miss Featherstone. And you, Lady Olivia, will you be bringing a beau?"

"No, I have no one to bring," said Olivia.

Glancing over her shoulder, she met Lord Sheridan's sardonic gaze. With a slight nod, he turned back to Lady Thorpe and made a comment. The entire group glanced at Olivia and laughed.

She turned completely and met his hard gaze without flinching. A moment passed and suddenly, that irresistible smile appeared. How could she help but answer it?

Then it was gone, and she was very sorry she had wasted a smile on such a cold fish. Olivia turned back to her dinner partner, catching the last of Tony's joke and laughing a bit too heartily.

She wanted very much to glance at the irritating Lord Sheridan and toss her head at him in disdain, but somehow, she knew the gesture would serve no purpose. How could she ignite a spark of remorse in such a heartless man?

More friends joined their small group, and Olivia soon forgot Lord Sheridan and his little band of misanthropists. Before she knew it, dinner was over. Mr. Pendleton, having begged the honor of sitting out the next dance with her and her aunt, led them back to the ballroom.

After a few minutes of quiet conversation, Aunt Amy looked longingly at the card room.

"I believe your aunt is wanting to play another hand of cards, Lady Olivia. Would you be insulted if I escorted her to the card room?"

"You two run along. I am promised for the next set, and I shall be fine here on my own."

Rising, her aunt said, "If you are certain, my dear."

Mr. Pendleton rose, too, and offered his arm to her aunt.

Olivia's toe tapped out the beat of the music, and she smiled as she watched the dancers. Tony was partnering one of their other friends, and they nodded as they passed.

"I fear I owe you an apology, Lady Olivia."

She started at the sound of his voice and choked. Clearing her throat, she said, "I cannot imagine why, Lord Sheridan."

He lifted the tails of his coat to join her on the bench but hesitated. "May I?"

She moved her skirts, and he sat down, carefully placing his gold-handled cane against his leg before he said, "I was rude in the dining room. I found it so odd that you and old Pendleton seemed to be getting on so well."

"Odd? There were several of us dining together and enjoying a pleasant conversation."

"Yes, but when you look around at one of these things, these balls, it is uncommon to see a wealthy older man courting a wealthy young lady."

Olivia shook her head and chuckled. "Courting? It was hardly a case of courtship. Even if it were, the alliance of two wealthy households is nothing out of the common. I think you must live in a very different world from me, my lord."

"No, I simply see my world for what it is—filled with people who wed for money or position, people who will step over a starving man and never notice he is there. I live in a very cold and indifferent world. Why do you think all these people are here tonight?"

When she didn't answer, he continued, "They are here because they want something. They want to better their own position in this avaricious society we live in."

"I cannot agree."

"Not agree? Then you are either a fool or blind, my dear lady. Only look at the tableau spread before you. That young lady there, dancing with an old reprobate like Lord Lowell. And there, the penniless Lord Fairhaven with the fish-faced but infinitely wealthy Miss Peabody."

Olivia's eyes flashed with passion, and she said, "Not everyone is avaricious. Perhaps you are judging others by your own standards." His jaw tightened, but he said nothing, and she continued, "Myself, I have friends in all circumstances—from the very wealthy to the very poor. I make no distinction."

He was scowling again, a much more familiar expression, thought Olivia. She resisted the urge to soothe him, but she did smile up at him to soften her words.

This seemed to have the desired effect as he said, "Then I must beg your pardon for judging you too harshly. I do hope you will forgive me." Again that fatal smile.

"Certainly." He rose, and she could not stop herself from adding, "You really should smile more often, Lord Sheridan. You have a very nice smile."

The smile faded, and he walked away, shaking his head.

What an odd man. She wished there were something she could do to help him. No one should be so cynical. It poisoned the soul, and she was certain that was the cause of his unhappiness.

Or perhaps, she thought, he had been disappointed in love. She knew hers was something of a romantic soul, but it was possible that someone had broken the disagreeable marquess's heart. Surely he could not still be grieving over a wife who died ten years past.

She turned to watch him converse with his friends, and a smile played on her lips. In that moment, Olivia vowed to help the Marquess of Sheridan find happiness again. She had had some experience in matchmaking and with such a handsome specimen, she felt confident that she would be able to hit upon the right young lady to make him smile again.

"Did you enjoy your tête-à-tête with Lady Olivia?" asked Sir Richard when Drew returned to his side.

"I do not know why I bothered to try and have a rational conversation with that female. She has only the most tenuous grasp on sensible thought."

"I found her delightful when I escorted her and her aunt home last night."

"And why the devil did you do that? Surely it was enough that I carried the limp Miss Featherstone to safety."

"You merely took care of their physical needs. I, on the other hand, saw to their spiritual needs. I soothed their ruffled feathers, a service requiring the utmost finesse, I might add, and after you finished with the beautiful Lady Olivia, hers were very ruffled indeed. Not that I expect you to understand something that you are incapable of doing."

"If you mean I am not capable of catering to the megrims and whims of three empty-headed females, then I can only say hurrah!" replied Drew.

Laughing, Sir Richard said, "I would accuse you of protesting too much where the beautiful, if empty-headed, Olivia is concerned, but I know that is not true. I take it you will not mind if I try my hand with the lady."

"Mind? I welcome it! I do not understand it, but I wish you well."

"Then I shall see what I can do to once again soothe those beautiful feathers that you so enjoy ruffling."

Sir Richard skirted the ballroom in his quest of Lady Olivia. His dark eyes narrowed, Drew watched with derision. When the lady greeted his friend with a warm smile, Drew ground his teeth. When she moved her skirts for Richard to join her on the velvet bench, just as she had for him moments earlier, Drew growled. Finally, when she placed her gloved hand on Richard's sleeve and leaned closer, Drew clutched his cane in his fist and strode out of the ballroom and out the front door without so much as a by-your-leave for his host or hostess.

CHAPTER FOUR

Two days later, when the sun finally put in an appearance again, Drew dressed for riding and went to Sir Richard's bachelor quarters.

"Where are you going?" asked the marquess when he entered his friend's bedchamber and discovered Richard's valet easing him into his coat.

"I have an engagement," said Sir Richard, "with a lady."

"So I gathered. You do not usually dress so fine for a visit to the club. Do I know her?"

"Oh yes, but I hesitate to mention her name, knowing how you feel about her, old friend."

Drew's dark brows came together, and he said coldly, "Lady Olivia. I might have known." He watched as his friend splashed on a liberal dose of cologne. "An assignation, is it?"

Sir Richard shook his head. "No, I fear it will be a rather large group. A picnic in the country, or some such boring interlude. However, one must pay one's dues in order to win the prize."

Drew frowned and said, "The prize being?"

"Lady Olivia's virtue, of course. I cannot be certain that it is, uh, intact, but if rumor is correct . . ." said Sir Richard with a leer.

"So this is not a private party."

"Certainly it is, but Lady Olivia assured me that I would be more than welcome."

"When did she say this?" asked Drew.

"Yesterday, when I was calling on her and her aunt. She also told me to bring along any friends I might wish to include. I had thought to invite you and Maddie, but she is busy and you . . . I assumed you would not wish to go."

The marquess could not guess what vagary of thought prompted him to say, "On the contrary, I would like nothing better. Shall we?"

Once spoken, he could not take it back without appearing a complete jinglebrains. Kicking himself mentally, Drew held open the door and waited for his friend to pass through.

He glanced down at his riding gear and added, "Will you ride or join the ladies in the carriage?"

"It's the carriage for me. My man thinks it looks like rain, and I would hate to ruin my new coat."

"Dandy," said Drew.

"Curmudgeon," said Sir Richard cheerfully.

Olivia donned her new bonnet with the blue ribbons that perfectly matched her riding habit and her eyes. She studied her reflection a moment and then smiled.

Seeing her maid in the mirror, she said, "Pansy,

you should be in bed! You are not strong enough to resume your duties."

"I am much better, m'lady," said the maid, picking up a pair of kid gloves.

Olivia took the gloves from her and said firmly, "Better, but not well. Mr. Jenson is coming to see you again this morning. He will kick up a dust if he finds you working already. Now, go back to bed, do."

"Very well, m'lady. If you insist."

"I do. He should be here any moment, and I want him to find you tucked up in your bed, a fire in the grate, and some warm broth by your side." Olivia tempered this lecture with a smile and shooed the little maid out the door.

A few minutes later, her aunt's maid entered and announced the good doctor's arrival.

"Take him up to see Pansy. I will be there in a few minutes. Is my aunt ready for the picnic?"

"Yes, my lady."

A few moments later, Olivia hurried out the door and up the back stairs. She found Mr. Jenson just leaving Pansy's room.

"Good morning, Mr. Jenson."

"Good morning, Lady Olivia. I am astounded at your maid's recovery. If I didn't know better, I would accuse her of having feigned her illness. She did not, of course."

"I am surprised, too. Only three days ago, she was practically at death's door."

"She is begging to return to her duties, but I told her to wait two more days and then, to be cautious. If she tires, she is to stop and rest."

"Thank you, Mr. Jenson. I hope I can convince her to follow your advice. Won't you come down to the drawing room for a cup of tea?"

"That would be very nice. Will your aunt be joining us?"

"I don't know. We are going on a picnic in a little while. I . . . I don't suppose you would like to join us, would you?"

"A picnic? I don't know. I have two or three patients to see today." The tall, distinguished-looking man frowned and finally nodded. "I suppose I have the time. Thank you, I will gladly accept your invitation."

"Excellent, and here is Aunt Amy, ready to go. The good doctor has agreed to lend us his company for the picnic, aunt. Why don't the two of you go into the drawing room and have some tea while I take care of a few last-minute details with the luncheon?"

Olivia stopped around the corner and listened.

"I hope you don't mind, Amy," he said.

"No, why should I mind? Come in. Witchell has already placed the tray in the drawing room."

Olivia smiled and turned toward the kitchens for a last-minute consultation with Cook over the quantity of food she was sending along. A knock sounded on the front door, and Olivia waited to see who was calling.

Witchell turned toward her and announced, "Lord Sheridan and Sir Richard, my lady."

Going forward with her hand extended, Olivia managed a composed, "Sir Richard, how good to see you again. And you have brought along Lord Sheridan."

"I hope you do not mind, Lady Olivia," said the charming Sir Richard with a wink.

Ignoring this familiarity, Olivia smiled broadly and declared, "Certainly not. You know that I said you should bring your other friends. Good afternoon, Lord Sheridan."

"Good afternoon, Lady Olivia," he replied. "Thank you for including me."

"Not at all. I am delighted you could come. Won't you follow me to the drawing room?"

So the marquess had agreed to come, thought Olivia. She had not been at all certain that he would accept his friend's invitation. Olivia smiled. She hoped Lord Sheridan would take a fancy to one of the two young ladies she had invited.

She was a fool, perhaps, to engage in all this matchmaking. It had not been enough that Mr. Pendleton would escort her aunt. Now she had added the good doctor. And for the marquess, two very pretty young ladies to choose from.

Making a moue, Olivia wished for a moment that someone would be so kind as to do a little matchmaking for her!

Twenty minutes later, the picnickers were on their way in two large traveling carriages and on horseback. Olivia turned her bay mare and fell in behind the first carriage. A moment later, the marquess joined her there.

"When we get out of the city, we should move ahead of the carriages, you know."

"And why should we do that, Lord Sheridan?" she asked.

"To avoid the dust, unless you enjoy eating the

dust kicked up by a team of horses and a lumbering carriage."

She laughed and shook her head, saying, "I enjoy cantering across a nice meadow of green grass, but I will settle for being in the lead of this caravan."

"Surprising," he muttered.

Olivia frowned and turned in her saddle to face him. "Why would you say that, my lord?"

"Only that I did not expect you to be so sensible."

"You have a very low opinion of me, my lord," she replied, thanking heaven that she had brought along Miss Featherstone's silly cousin and Miss Hollingsworth to entertain the maddening marquess. Misanthropist, indeed! He was nothing more than a smug coxcomb.

"You are put out with me, Lady Olivia—once again."

"I don't know what you are talking about, my lord. I have no opinion of you, one way or the other."

"Ah, and now you are lying. You are not very good at it, you know. Your eyes get very wide when you lie."

She turned her head away as her cheeks reddened, but she refused to reply. She had learned through the years that it did no good to argue with children or fools.

"A word to the wise, my lady. You should not play any card games where you must try to bluff your opponent. You would lose your fortune in a matter of minutes."

Turning her sweetest smile on him, she said, "I

would never dream of doing anything so foolish, Lord Sheridan. Isn't it a lovely day?"

That delicious smile appeared, and he said, "Perfectly lovely."

Just then, Mr. Thomas moved up to join them and said, "Let us move in front of the carriages."

"A capital idea," said Lord Sheridan, kicking up his horse and moving ahead.

Olivia followed with Mr. Thomas and Miss Hollingsworth, who had also chosen to ride.

Allowing the two gentlemen to ride ahead, Olivia said, "A handsome man, Lord Sheridan."

"He is well enough," said the young lady. "Mama says he is worth a fortune, and that, of course, makes him acceptable. Still and all, he is rather old. I mean, he might be quite suitable for you, my lady, but for me?"

Olivia sucked in a quick breath of air as if hit in the stomach. Glancing sideways, she managed a smile but said, "In time, Miss Hollingsworth, I believe you will find that age is not as important as wisdom."

The young lady flipped her long curls in disdain and said, "But you only say that, Lady Olivia, because you have both. This is only my second Season, and I have no desire to settle for someone almost twice my age."

"Perfectly understandable," said Olivia. "Shall we join the gentlemen?" Clicking her tongue, she sent her mare forward to catch up with the two gentlemen.

So much for the pretty Miss Hollingsworth, thought Olivia. Perhaps Miss Featherstone's cousin, Miss

Fallon, would prove more suitable for the handsome marquess. Olivia glanced at his profile and admitted to herself that she did find him very handsome. He was not a youth, just as Miss Hollingsworth had said, but the man was hardly in his dotage. The silvering of his dark hair at the temples only added to his elegance, rather than detracted from it. If he would smile more often . . .

She heaved a sigh—too loudly, as it attracted the marquess's attention. He turned to her, and his dark eyes were intent but not sardonic. He didn't smile, but his eyes changed subtly, the corners crinkling in amusement. Olivia stared, forgetting her mare for a moment, and the beast sidestepped daintily, causing Olivia to grab at the pommel.

The marquess's hand shot out, effortlessly bringing the little mare under control.

"Thank you, Lord Sheridan."

"Not at all, Lady Olivia. Perhaps you would do better in one of the carriages until we have left behind the hustle and bustle of the city."

Flushing uncomfortably, Olivia said, "I am fine. My attention merely strayed for a few seconds."

Olivia chastised herself silently—not for forgetting her surroundings, but for having such kindly thoughts toward the cynical marquess. He was not the sort of man she could care for, not even on the best of days. He was much too superior for her taste. Miss Fallon, however, was just an impressionable girl in her first Season. She shouldn't mind having someone tell her what to do all the time.

"Lady Olivia, Miss Hollingsworth and I were wondering exactly where it is that we are going?" asked Mr. Thomas.

"Mr. Pendleton is leading us to a quiet little spot on his estate near Richmond. It shouldn't take too long to get there."

"How is it you know Pendleton?" asked the marquess.

"I was friends with his late wife. Such a tragedy. He took it so hard. I am pleased to see that he is rejoining Society this Season."

"Why would he not? He still has need of a broodmare."

"Lord Sheridan! Your conversation is not only unsuitable, it is also quite heartless! How can you say such a thing?"

"I say it because it is the truth. Pendleton needs an heir. How else is he to get one without marrying a young woman all over again—just like last time. I assumed that was why you sought him out."

"That is insulting to both me and my late friend! What is more, it is untrue! Suzannah cared for Mr. Pendleton."

"For his money, you mean. I hear the marriage settlement pulled that foolish brother of hers out of the River Tick just in time. And as for her mother's extravagance at the dressmaker . . ."

"Nevertheless, Suzannah cared very deeply. . . ."

"Yes, yes, that is what they always say. But I ask you, would your friend have married Pendleton if he had been penniless?"

The marquess dropped back then to ride beside one of the carriages, conversing with the people inside for a moment. Olivia, still fuming, could not have managed speech if her life depended on it. She had known the marquess was cynical, but his attitude was positively disparaging of his own class. How he could bear to be a part of something he so despised, she could not imagine. How hypocritical of the man!

Olivia vowed to have nothing to do with him for the remainder of the day! He could just take those broad shoulders and that handsome face and find someone else to annoy!

"I don't know why I let you talk me into coming today," muttered Drew while he frowned at his friend. They passed the tables and chairs that had been set up for the picnic and strolled toward the others.

"Talk you into it? Why, you practically begged to come along! Don't blame me if you and Lady Olivia cannot play nice together."

"Hell and blast! She is the most infuriating female. The look she gave me for merely telling her the truth about Pendleton and his young wife!"

"Suzannah Humphries? I understand from Miss Hepplewhite that Olivia and Suzannah were the best of friends. No wonder she did not wish to hear your usual complaints. I tell you, Drew, you must learn to play by the rules if you wish to be included in Society's games—for your daughter's sake, if not your own."

Sir Richard moved away to speak to the pretty Lady Olivia and Miss Featherstone, Lord Hardcastle's new fiancée. Drew ground his teeth and glared at the entire assemblage. For tuppence, he would have mounted his gelding and ridden away. No one would have missed him. They were absorbed in their childish games of croquet and archery.

"Come and sit with me, Lord Sheridan," said Lady Olivia's aunt. She patted the chair by her side, and he obediently joined her. "I know when one has a picnic, one is supposed to recline on the ground on blankets, but I am too old for that. I am so glad Mr. Pendleton had his people come out and set up tables and chairs so that we could dine as civilized folks."

She glanced at him and raised her brow. "This is the part where you tell me that I am not at all old, that you are delighted to sit with me instead of joining those annoying children over there who are playing croquet."

Chuckling, Drew said, "And do you always want gentlemen to state the obvious, Miss Hepplewhite?"

"Oh, I knew I would like you! Hand me that plate of macaroons, won't you? I intend to eat only sweets today. That is my reward for coming outside and sitting in the open all day. I do so hate picnics," she added.

"Now that I know you feel that way, I think we shall rub along very well together, Miss Hepplewhite."

"Oh, do call me Amy. Miss Hepplewhite is such a mouthful. And yes, I know it is not at all the thing, but it will do me the world of good to have such a handsome man call me by my given name."

"Very well. Amy, it shall be, and you shall call me Sheri."

"How very wicked of us, Sheri," said the older woman, downing her glass of wine and holding it out for him to fill again. "Only look at that silly Mr. Jenson. A physician, you know, and yet you would never guess the way he is concentrating on that shot he is about to make. There! Muffed it, he did. He always was a bit of a clunch!"

"I have heard of Mr. Jenson. I believe he has an excellent reputation in the medical world."

"What has that to say to the matter?" she replied, turning and staring at him for a moment. "I ask you, what good is it being such a bright fellow in the medical world if you go and make micefeet of all the rest of your life?"

"Would you like another macaroon, Amy?" he asked, handing the entire platter to her.

She took one, and he looked about him for more food that might appeal to his strange new friend. Obviously, she was not accustomed to drinking great quantities, and the lack of food coupled with Pendleton's excellent wine must have made her light-headed. To his surprise, he found her very amusing and didn't wish for her to say anything she might regret.

"These little meat pasties are wonderful," he said, handing her two.

She put one in her mouth and smiled at him. After swallowing, she said, "I am not usually so talkative, my lord. And I am not as disguised as you think. I am just in a foul mood, though I have no intention of explaining the why and wherefore. I do apologize, my lord."

"No apology necessary, Amy. And I thought you were to call me Sheri."

"Perhaps, when we are not surrounded by the children," she said with a laugh. "Even my sweet Olivia would not approve of such an arrangement, and she likes everyone and everything."

"Yes, I had noticed that about her. Does she

never frown? Even when I made her mad on the way here, she merely stopped talking. She should have railed at me."

"She is like that—sweet to the very core."

"But surely there are things that anger her. One cannot be forever smiling and gay."

"The things that upset her are the things of life, and she prefers fixing the ones she can without talking about it."

Drew would have questioned Amy about her cryptic remarks, but just then, they were joined by Mr. Jenson.

"I had to leave the game of croquet to the younger ones," said Mr. Jenson, sitting down at the table. "My back just won't permit me to bend in that uncomfortable manner."

Drew wanted to laugh at the frosty reception Mr. Jenson received from Miss Hepplewhite. He put her age at near fifty, but she was twisting the good doctor into knots like the most accomplished coquette.

Taking pity on the man, Drew said, "I don't believe we have met formally, Mr. Jenson, though I know your reputation. I am Sheridan."

"How do you do, my lord? Isn't it fine weather we are having today? Perfect for a picnic."

"Splendid weather. Don't you agree, Amy?" he said, earning a chuckle from the irrepressible Miss Hepplewhite.

"Yes, quite splendid, Sheri," she replied, touching her gloved hand to his sleeve with a smile.

The doctor's brows rose, and his chest puffed out. Drew would have felt sorry for him, but he was enjoying himself too much to stop. He wasn't

certain why Amy Hepplewhite was torturing Mr.
Jenson, but he had no desire to spoil her fun.

The others finished their games of croquet and
archery and returned to the tables for refreshments. Richard, with Lady Olivia on his arm, lin-
gered near the archery set, his head close to hers.

As they came closer, Drew turned to Miss
Featherstone's cousin and said, "Miss Fallon, you
must try the meat pasties. Let me serve you."

She giggled and accepted his offering, gazing
up at him with soulful eyes. He knew it was his turn
to say something witty, to offer her a compliment,
but his momentary lapse of good sense had fled,
and he said nothing. A moment later, she turned
away.

Hell and blast, he thought. *Now everyone will think
I'm nothing but a tongue-tied youth, moonstruck by her
beauty.*

"Lord Sheridan, you can give me another one of
those," said Miss Hepplewhite.

"Certainly. Is there anything else you require?
Another glass of wine?"

"No, no, I have plenty, thank you. Mr. Pendleton,
a perfect setting for a magnificent picnic."

"First rate, sir," said Drew, raising his glass. "To
our host, Mr. Pendleton."

Everyone toasted the old man, who rose and
said a few words of welcome. Drew did not bother
to listen. His mind was meandering into unfamiliar
territory as he watched his friend hook arms with
Lady Olivia as they sipped from their glasses. This
caused a frenzy of copycats as the younger people
did the same. Even the sensible Miss Hepplewhite

was persuaded by the good doctor to attempt this feat.

Once again, Drew felt the veriest outsider. Not that he minded, he told himself. He preferred his solitary state. He had never planned to be otherwise.

Still, when Lady Olivia threw back her head and laughed, he felt his stomach twist as a wave of envy for his friend swept over him. Her skin was like porcelain and her cheeks were dusty pink. He had never seen a more beautiful woman.

"Lord Sheridan, you are not drinking?" asked the doctor.

Drew started. Glancing at the glass, poised for a drink but forgotten, he drained it and set it on the table. Without a word, he filled his plate and set to eating.

Odd, he thought, *how Mr. Pendleton's repast suddenly has the consistency of sawdust.*

After everyone had had their fill, they drifted back to play croquet or take a walk. Lord Hardcastle and Miss Featherstone took a blanket and wandered away to sit together under an oak tree. Mr. Pendleton had secured Lady Olivia and was strolling toward the stream. Without hurrying, Drew followed.

He wasn't eavesdropping, but he could not have ignored Lady Olivia's quiet gasp of excitement. The thought that the old miser might be asking for her hand sent a cold shiver up his spine, and he walked a little faster.

Mr. Pendleton, flustered by the hug she had bestowed on him, was blushing a fiery red and stammering without saying anything coherent.

"Is everything all right?" asked Drew, covering his suspicion with concern.

"No, no, my lord. That is, Lady Olivia is only a little excited by my suggestion."

"Am I to congratulate you?" he asked faintly.

"Only on Mr. Pendleton's generous gift," exclaimed Lady Olivia. "I wanted him to give me some money for a charity of mine. Instead, he has offered us land for our school. The land we stand on right now!"

The old man shook his head and said, "It is nothing. Besides, what am I to do with it? As they say, you cannot take it with you—money or land."

"Still, it is so generous of you. You will not be sorry, sir. And we will call it . . . Pendleton School."

"Really, my lady. Quite unnecessary . . . quite . . . oh, well, if you insist. I suppose that would be all right."

"I do insist," said Lady Olivia, placing a chaste kiss on the man's wrinkled cheek. His color deepened, and he excused himself and hurried away, leaving Drew alone with Lady Olivia.

"I didn't mean to intrude," he said.

"You didn't, I was just so surprised. Mr. Pendleton is not known for his generosity, but it is such a good cause."

"Perhaps he is trying to impress you," said Drew, not thinking before speaking.

"I might have known you would question his motives," she said.

"No, I didn't mean . . . that is, I do not think that at all, Lady Olivia. I apologize." He smiled at her, and she seemed to soften. Taking her arm and strolling away from the others, he said, "Just who will go to this school? Girls from good families, I suppose."

"No, no, it will be in part an orphanage—a home for children who either have no parents or have parents who have failed them. Right now, the school is in the City—a location that doesn't allow for the children to play outside like they should."

"And the other part?" At her puzzled frown, he added, "You said that the school will be an orphanage in part. What is the other part?"

"We have several children whose parents cannot afford them at this time. Their mothers are alive— some are soldiers' widows, but they cannot afford to keep their children with them. This home will allow the mothers and children to be together again—I hope. It depends on how much money it will take, but I envision small cottages for the mothers with children and then a larger building, a dormitory, for the orphans and abandoned children. They will be so much happier here!" she added. With a gurgle of laughter, she twirled around in delight, her arms open wide.

Drew smiled at her. "I fear I may have misjudged you, Lady Olivia."

She stopped and stared, a slight frown wrinkling her brow. "In what way, Lord Sheridan?"

"I had no idea you cared about anyone except Society and all its frivolity. Again, I apologize."

"And again, your apology is accepted. Perhaps now you will not think so poorly of us."

"Is that what you think? You think that I look down on everyone else?"

"Don't you?"

His expression had lost all trace of lightness as

he replied, "I suppose I do, my lady. I have seen little in Society that has earned my admiration. Oh, beauty and grace, but with a hollow core. You may not see it. Perhaps one has to have lived away from it for a few years. For me, I married quite young, and the part of Society I took to my home, to my bed, was nothing to admire."

"I am sorry," she whispered.

"So was I, but I had no one to blame but myself. I was naive. I did not understand Society at that time."

"If you despise Society so much, why come to London for the Season?"

His crack of laughter held no mirth, only self-mockery. "I have my daughter to consider. She will be seventeen next year. She will expect her own Season, and I have not the will to deny it to her. I only hope that she will be wiser than I was."

He turned and walked away. This time, he stopped to bid his host and Miss Hepplewhite good-bye. Then Drew mounted his horse and returned to London.

CHAPTER FIVE

How her heart ached for him! Olivia had done nothing all evening except worry about the taciturn Lord Sheridan. If he had remained with her another minute, she was certain she would have thrown her arms around him to comfort him—and what a disaster that would have been! It would have convinced the uncompromising marquess that she really was addlepated.

And that, much to Olivia's surprise, was not at all what she wanted him to think of her.

On this disturbing reflection, Olivia turned over in her bed and punched the pillow into shape. She flopped over again and tried to settle in for sleep—an impossible undertaking. After several minutes of thinking very diligently about the tasks she had set herself to accomplish the next day, her mind returned to Lord Sheridan.

He really was a stubborn man!

Very well, she thought, sitting up in the bed and lighting the candle on the table. She picked up a small notebook and opened it. Taking out the pencil tucked inside, she was ready to begin her list of eligible young ladies, suitable young ladies, young ladies worthy of the Marquess of Sheridan.

Five minutes later, Olivia set the pencil aside, staring in wonder at the words she had doodled while waiting for inspiration to strike.

Lady Olivia Sheridan.

"I tell you, Fitz, I was fairly thunderstruck when I heard about Lady Olivia Cunningham's school. There she was talking about raising funds to build the thing, and I never opened my mouth about helping."

"That is not like you, your lordship," said his secretary from his station behind the battered desk that had belonged to Drew's father.

At the sideboard in the library, Drew poured himself a large brandy before strolling across the room and sitting down in front of the desk. His secretary closed the ledger he was working on and took out a sheet of paper to receive his instructions for the day.

Drew, however, was in a reflective mood and didn't notice. After a moment, he said, "No, it is not like me. I made a cake of myself, but I intend to remedy that. I want you to find out all you can about her school—the one she has now is in London— and then I want you to find a way that I may donate to it."

"Without her knowing?"

"Precisely."

Fitzsimmons scribbled a few words on the paper

and then looked up, waiting for further instructions.

Drew sipped his brandy and then said, "Find out about any charities she's involved with. Go to Bow Street, and get Butters to help. He can go 'round to her house and question the servants. You have the address from when you sent those flowers for me, don't you?"

Fitzsimmons opened a drawer and pulled out a small sheet of paper. Drew took it and read it before handing it back again.

Then he continued, "Good, good. Butters can talk to the servants then. They always know more about what is going on than anybody else."

"I'll contact him immediately, my lord."

"Good." Seeing the look of bewilderment in his secretary's eyes, Drew said gruffly, "If I have misjudged the lady, then she probably has other causes she could use help with, though the school is the main one I am interested in. Helping orphans and abandoned children. And the widows of our soldiers, too. Now that is something I admire."

Drew rose, tossed off the contents of his glass, and then strolled to the door. The secretary let his pencil fall as the marquess opened the door and left the room.

Drew picked up his hat and gloves from the table in the hall and went out. He ambled along the pavement, not caring which direction he took as his mind worked on various problems—mostly those related to Lady Olivia Cunningham.

It was her charity work that interested him, of course. Whereas he contributed to a number of charities around his estate at home, she worked here, in London. He had written off this particular portion of the country years earlier. There had seemed no hope for helping London's poor and misfortunate. It was a job too overwhelming to succeed. To his way of thinking, no amount of money would have helped, but Lady Olivia was making it work, evidently. On the one hand, he admired her for it. On the other, there was a callous part of him that wanted to deride her efforts as foolish and impotent. It was this part of him that ruled his life when he was in London, and he found it difficult to check.

For the marquess, to be thought a fool was the worst sort of insult—an insult his young wife had hurled at his head every time he had tried to fix the problems that plagued their marriage. Now that had been an impossible task!

No, he prided himself on always being rational. He avoided not only doing foolish things but also foolish people. To think he might be playing a fool now was completely unacceptable. He would have to be cautious. If Lady Olivia's ventures were foolish, then he wanted no part of them. If not, then he would support her completely—if anonymously.

You're a coward, he thought. *You want to help, but only if it suits your rigid code of behavior. What does it matter if she fails? At least she is trying.*

Drew glanced around him, getting his bearings. He had wandered away from his usual neighborhood, and now he found himself in a street off Grosvenor Square. The houses were large and set back from the street enough to have narrow flower beds along the pavement.

He read the number of the house in front of

him. Number eight. Something, some inner devil, had brought him to her house. He almost turned to flee.

A carriage pulling up behind him prevented his departure. The door opened, and Miss Hepplewhite descended.

"Is that you, Lord Sheridan? Have you come to call? I do hope so." She took his arm and said, "I have just left Maria Sefton, and she is under the weather. Most distressing, I can tell you. I need a handsome gentleman to take my mind off her. Do come into the drawing room and wait for me while I take off this bonnet and coat."

The room was definitely feminine. The carpets were a riot of pink and cream-colored roses. The paper on the walls was a striped pink and cream. The furnishings were in various shades of rose and green and were delicately carved. Still, it was a comfortable room. A basket by the sofa held a stack of mending. On the table at the other end of the sofa was a small stand with an unfinished needlework project. A sheet of music lay on the bench by a well-used pianoforte. Drew crossed the room and picked out the melody—a ballad about love lost.

"Good afternoon, your lordship. Miss Hepplewhite thought you might be hungry so I have brought the tea tray in for you. If you prefer a glass of ale, I have some very good stock in the library."

"Tea will be fine. Thank you, uh . . ."

"Witchell, my lord." The butler poured the cup of tea and then straightened. "Will there be anything else, your lordship?"

"No, that will be all." The butler retreated but turned when Drew asked, "Is Lady Olivia at home?"

"No, my lord. She has gone out for the day."

"I see."

He sat down to his tea, helping himself to a small cake and placing it on a dainty porcelain plate. He had finished one portion and was considering a second when a breathless Miss Hepplewhite sailed into the room.

Drew half rose, but she shooed him back into his seat.

"What has Witchell managed for us this afternoon? Ah, some macaroons. I could eat my weight in them every day."

"A small portion, to be sure," said Drew, placing two on her plate.

She grinned at him and said, "I never knew what a complete hand you were, Lord Sheridan."

"Sheri, remember?"

"Yes, yes, it is Sheri, when we are private."

"And in public, you must call me Sheridan. All my best friends do so."

"Then so shall I. Let's see. That makes three of us here in London, does it not?"

He frowned at the impertinence, but she was still favoring him with a warm smile, and he nodded. "Yes, a total of three—unless my mother should venture to Town. An unlikely event, I can tell you."

"The dowager prefers the country?"

"Yes, as far from any other people as she can get. My mother has turned into a bit of a hermit."

"She was never very social, as I recall," said Amy, stirring her tea thoughtfully.

"You knew my mother when she was younger?"

"Yes, we met on occasion. You are very like her."

"Hardly," said Drew. "She is fair and was blond, before her hair turned gray."

"No, not your looks. I meant your personality. The dowager marchioness didn't seem to enjoy being here in London very much either."

Drew frowned. This conversation was becoming much too personal. It was time he put paid to Miss Hepplewhite's impertinence.

Lifting his quizzing glass, he stared at her a moment and then said, "Sometimes, there is very little to enjoy here in London."

She laughed, a tinkling sound that was quite as infectious as her smile. She put a hand on his sleeve and leaned closer, saying, "Oh, that is very good! I don't believe I have ever seen anyone use a quizzing glass to such advantage. Were I a mushroom, I would be quaking in my boots!"

Drew smiled and shook his head. "You are an extraordinary woman, Miss Hepplewhite."

"Amy," she said.

"Amy. That look is guaranteed to depress the intentions of the most encroaching toady. But as you say, as you are not one . . ."

"Well, among friends, one can say what one pleases. I am all for the rules our Society has set out for us, but I am not going to follow them in my own home. Well, Olivia's home."

Drew looked about him as if expecting Olivia to materialize. "Are you expecting Lady Olivia soon?"

"Goodness no. She and that gorilla of hers have gone out to . . . to check on certain business concerns."

He could tell she was hedging her bets, but he

didn't wish to be too openly interested, so he changed his tact and asked, "Gorilla?"

"Her servant. A former prizefighter. He is a decent man and a loyal servant, but he does nothing for her aura."

"Aura?"

"Yes, you know. The way she appears to others."

"Something that does not matter very much to me," he replied.

"Of course it does," said the older woman, her frustration showing on her face. "You care very much about it. For instance, why do you carry that quizzing glass? And the cane you take everywhere? What purpose does it serve? You are certainly not lame, Sheri."

"No, I am not," he replied, his words clipped. This conversation was getting out of hand.

She heaved a sigh and sat back, relaxing against the back of the sofa as no proper lady would do. Miss Hepplewhite felt very comfortable with him indeed, and this went far to erase his irritation. He waited for her next salvo. It didn't take long.

Leaning forward again, Amy said, "You carry the quizzing glass—a little outdated, perhaps, but you do it so well—and the cane because you are trying to present a certain image of yourself. For you to suddenly appear without them would be like a knight of old appearing without his armor. It simply isn't done. The world, as we know it, would collapse if the Marquess of Sheridan came to a ball, sans cane, and actually danced!"

She heaved a sigh and relaxed against the green velvet cushions once again. Drew smiled. Then he chuckled, and finally he laughed—a sound that filled the room. Rising, he swept her a deep bow.

"If I had my hat on, I would doff it to you, my dear Miss Hepplewhite—Amy. For someone who has only recently come within my sphere of influence, you have read my character remarkably well. Bravo!"

He sat down, lifted her hand to his lips, and kissed it. At that moment, the door opened, and the butler announced Mr. Jenson.

The doctor hesitated before entering. Then he said, "Good morning, Lord Sheridan, Miss Hepplewhite." Crossing the room, he bowed before them.

"Good morning, Mr. Jenson," said Drew.

"Are you here to see Pansy again?" asked Amy.

"What? No, that is, yes. I . . . I thought I would just check on my patient."

"She is probably in Olivia's room. Have Witchell take you to her."

The man opened his mouth to speak, then thought better of it and shuffled out the door.

When it closed, Drew said, "Why do you torture that poor fellow so?"

"It is nothing more than he deserves," she replied. Then she clamped her lips tightly together to indicate that that was all she had to say on the subject.

Drew rose to leave, but before he could speak, the butler entered again.

"Mr. Pendleton."

"Good morning, Mr. Pendleton. Do come in and join us," said his hostess.

Drew had no choice but to sit down again. With a nod, he said, "Pendleton."

"Good morning, Miss Hepplewhite, Lord Sheridan."

"Would you care for some tea?"

"Yes, thank you. I have just come from the solicitors. Is Lady Olivia here?"

"No, she and her henchman have gone out. I don't expect her home for hours. Where she gets the energy, I cannot imagine. Was it something urgent?"

"Not at all. I merely wanted to tell her . . ." He hesitated, glancing at Drew. Then he shrugged and said, "I suppose it doesn't matter as you were there the other day anyway. I have just signed the papers to deed over that bit of land for Lady Olivia's school."

"Has she the funds to build it?" asked Drew.

"I don't know. I plan to give her something toward the building, and I know she always gives, too, but I have no idea where the rest of the money will come from. I only know that what Lady Olivia sets out to do, she does," said the old man.

Just then, the doctor returned to the room. Drew rose and indicated his vacated seat.

"Come and take my seat, Mr. Jenson. I really should be going." He bowed over Amy's hand and turned to grin up at her. She rolled her eyes heavenward but said nothing.

"Good afternoon, gentlemen."

"Lord Sheridan," they said in reply.

Drew was whistling this time as he walked along. It was odd that the boredom that so often overtook him when in London had vanished. In its place was a sense of purpose, a sense of pleasure and expectation.

Drew continued his ambles, this time heading toward his tailor, Weston's, on Conduit Street. There he ordered a new waistcoat in a daring bishop's blue and a new riding coat, too. For a member of the *ton*, Drew spent remarkably little time on his wardrobe. His clothes were of excellent quality, but his color palette was invariably conservative. The blue brocade waistcoat would seem a little out of place in his cupboard.

From Weston's, he continued on to Piccadilly. Here, he went into Hatchard's and stopped at the front desk. His daughter, Rebekah, had asked for the latest novels, and he wanted to surprise her with a package sent to her school. On a display stand near the door was a book about steam engines. On a whim, Drew had the clerk wrap this up, too, for Arthur at Eton. It was just the sort of thing his bookish son would devour.

As the marquess left the store, he stepped back to allow two giggling young ladies to enter with their maid. Tipping his hat, he was arrested by the sight of his friend Richard strolling along the pavement. The beautiful Lady Olivia was on his arm, laughing at something the rake had said.

There was nothing clandestine about the two. They were out in the open, in daylight. He couldn't help wondering what had brought them together. Miss Hepplewhite had said that Olivia was out for the day with her servant as a companion. There was no servant in sight. Not that there had to be for propriety's sake—not in the middle of Piccadilly, he reminded himself.

He had assumed she was out doing good works. He had assumed her errands were those of helping others. He had assumed entirely too much.

Drew turned toward home. He would write letters to his children and give the letters and the books to his secretary to post. There were several matters his secretary had been asking him to look into personally, so he would spend the rest of the afternoon attending to business.

Upon arriving home, he found a note from Sir Richard. He tossed it aside, then retrieved it. Opening the envelope, there was only a short message.

Sheri,
    Instead of going together, meet me at Vauxhall tonight. I have a few things to do first and will be running late.
Richard

Drew crumbled the note. He toyed with the idea of simply forgetting their engagement. No, he decided. He would meet Richard there. What reason could he give for not going? That he had been in the doldrums over seeing his friend with Lady Olivia?

That wasn't true, of course, he told himself. He had no reason to resent Richard and Lady Olivia going out together. He had been angered only at the thought that Miss Hepplewhite had dissembled to him, had led him to believe that her niece was out on business.

And that, if he examined his motives closely, was not really true either. Drew, who prided himself on being truthful with others to the point of bluntness, was now lying to himself.

But he didn't care, couldn't care, what Lady

Olivia did or did not do. And he certainly didn't care with whom!

Drew bowed his head as it began to throb.

Had the world gone mad, or was he the only one?

"Hell and blast!" he muttered.

Olivia arrived home with time to spare before dressing for dinner and her evening jaunts. She discovered her aunt prostrate on her bed, a cool cloth on her head.

"I cannot go out tonight, my dear. I feel far too weak."

"I am sorry, Aunt. I hope you are not sickening with what befell Pansy. Should I call Mr. Jenson?"

Her aunt sat bolt upright on her bed and said, "No! That is what started all this in the first place!" She fell back, and the feather mattress let out a little whoosh.

"Oh? You have the headache because of Mr. Jenson?" said Olivia, her tone teasing.

"No, not because of him. Rather it was because of entertaining him—and Mr. Pendleton. Do those two not realize I have other things to do than sit in the drawing room with the two of them looking daggers at each other?"

"Looking daggers? Daggers of jealousy," said Olivia with a giggle.

Her aunt glared at her. "You are not the only one with gentlemen callers, my girl."

"Certainly not, Aunt. I meant nothing by it. I hope you recover quickly from your indisposition."

"I shall be fine, dear. I merely have the headache—a particularly wicked one, but only a headache."

"Very well, I shall leave you to Jinks's ministrations." Olivia opened the door, but she couldn't resist one last quip. "Unless, of course, you need me to send for the doctor."

"Baggage!" said her aunt.

"Rest well, dearest," replied Olivia, blowing her aunt a kiss before shutting the door.

Olivia went downstairs and wandered out to the garden. It was a lovely place to sit in solitude. Large shrubs lined the walkways, hiding her from anyone who might be peering out the house windows. In the middle was an open patch of grass dotted with small flower beds. Here she discovered the three-legged dog, Hasty, playing with Hawkeye. The cat would race from one flower bed to the next, turning his head to the left so that with his one eye he could see the dog coming.

"You will have to do better than that," she said to the dog. He paused in his play and ran up to her, wagging his stubby tail with pleasure. "Good boy, Hasty. Now, go back to entertaining our friend. Tire him out so he will not want to play with my toes under the covers tonight."

As if he understood her, the dog trotted back to the flower bed where Hawkeye lay in wait. Springing into the air, the cat fled behind the next bed while the dog followed, repeating the same pattern again.

Olivia sat down on a stone bench to watch. A moment later, a shadow fell across her, and she looked up to find Harold waiting patiently.

"Yes, Harold?"

"Mr. Witchell said to give you this letter that Mr. Pendleton left for you."

"Thank you." He handed her the letter and turned to go, but she stopped him. "Harold, we are going out tonight."

"Yes, m'lady."

"To Vauxhall."

"Oh, m'lady, not that idea again. It's too dangerous."

"Not with you there. And we did rescue that one unfortunate girl."

"But you shouldn't be . . ."

"Now, Harold, would you deny others the chance to live a decent life? No, I thought not. I understand that in the dark pathways, there are any number of . . . ladies, looking for a . . . job. I plan to find those poor, wretched girls and help them."

"Very well," he said.

"And you may rid yourself of that hangdog look. I need your help, Harold."

"I still say it is too dangerous, my lady," he ventured.

His mistress, however, only nibbled her lip for a minute and then said, "True, I did find that part of it rather uncomfortable. Very well, then we will each take along a pistol. I will keep one in my reticule, and you shall carry one in your pocket. You remember how to use it, do you not?"

"Aye, Mr. Pate taught me just fine. Why don't we take Rattle with us? Better yet, what if I take Rattle, and we see what we can do by ourselves?"

"What? No, that would never work. The only thing you and Rattle alone would get is in trouble.

But it would be a good idea to take Rattle for extra protection. Yes, tell him for me and see to it that he is armed, too. Then it is all settled. My aunt is not feeling well, so tonight will be the perfect opportunity for us to find those girls in need of our help. We leave at nine."

"Yes, m'lady."

Dressed in black with only his snowy cravat lighting his appearance, Drew set out for Vauxhall to meet his friend. He made the short journey by carriage, arriving at the gates and sending the driver away. Carriages lined the street, their drivers and footmen clustered here and there as they waited for their wealthy masters and mistresses to return.

Passing a sleek landaulet, Drew frowned. The crest on the side looked familiar. He continued on his way, trying to remember where he had seen that particular crest. Then it dawned on him. It was the same as the crest on the huge traveling carriage that had taken guests to the picnic at Pendleton's estate. It was Lady Olivia's carriage.

Was it only a coincidence that Richard had invited him to Vauxhall this night? And was this the reason that Richard had not been able to travel to Vauxhall with him? Perhaps Lady Olivia was the thing that had occupied his friend all afternoon.

Drew frowned at these theories. He was becoming entirely too concerned with Lady Olivia. What if Olivia and Richard's meeting in the afternoon had led to an assignation this evening? It was no concern of his.

He continued on to the Rotunda, always looking for Richard. From there, he tried the walkway to the waterfall. There was still no sign of his friend. Grumbling in frustration while his stomach grumbled with hunger, Drew wandered through the darkened paths. He would give Richard another thirty minutes, and then he would leave.

Giggles and a deep voice made him take another direction. Before he knew it, he was quite turned around. The orchestra in the Rotunda was little more than a whine. He stopped and listened for a moment to get his bearings.

The moon had risen. When Drew turned a corner, he could see the silhouettes of two people in a small clearing ahead, both females. One was clad in an elegant gown, but the other was dressed in a gown that was almost transparent in the moonlight. An odd combination. Drew edged closer.

"I'm not doin' too bad fer m'self, your ladyship."

"I'm sure you are not, Mary, but there are better ways to earn a living. I can help you."

" 'Elp me t' live like me mum, scraping out a livin' and dyin' o' starvation? No thanks, says I."

"It will not be like that. I will see to it that you learn a skill, and while you are learning it, you will have a decent place to live."

Drew stepped closer, disbelief powering his feet. It was Lady Olivia, speaking to . . . but that was impossible! Surely she was not so foolish!

"Look, I have written my direction on this card. If you should change your mind, come to this address."

"I don't know. I . . ."

"What the devil is going on?" growled the marquess, stepping into the moonlight.

With a little screech, the girl vanished, leaving Lady Olivia alone to face him.

She bent to pick up the piece of paper. Shaking it, she stormed up to him and said, "Now look what you did! I almost had her!"

"Dash it all, woman, have you lost your senses?" he shouted.

"Dash it all yourself, sir! I am here on a mission of mercy, and you have seen fit to ruin it! There is no telling where that poor girl will end her days, thanks to you!"

She lifted her hand to slap his face, but he caught it handily.

Bringing his face close to hers, he spat out, "You don't want to add to your foolishness by doing that, my dear."

"Oh!" she yelped and stomped on his foot.

He threw her away from him. "Hellcat!"

"Overbearing popinjay!"

He grabbed her wrist and pulled her against his chest. "Have you no sense? Do you have no idea what kind of danger you are in, wandering these dark alleys alone?"

"I am not in any danger," she said.

"Oh? And what is to prevent some ugly customer from doing this?"

He kissed her, his lips rough on hers. She stiffened, twisting her head, but he held her in his grip and continued. Then she was kissing him back, her lips searching his, her arms around his neck, her fingers ruffling his hair. He tasted her sweetness and only wanted more. His arms wrapped around her, pressing the length of her body against him.

They staggered, and Drew set her away from him.

His senses reeling, he panted, "See? What is to prevent that? Or worse!"

Her eyes were glazed, and she bit at her lower lip in the most provocative manner. Drew restrained himself from reaching for her again, but his anger was reasserting itself, and he resisted temptation.

His breathing almost normal again, he demanded, "Well, what do you have to say for yourself?"

The fire returned to her eyes, and she said, "Harold!" Drew took a step back when a large figure stepped into the light. Behind this giant was another, a youth also dressed in livery.

"What I have to say, Lord Sheridan, is that if you had been a ruffian, Harold and Rattle would have knocked you flat!"

She signaled to the servants, and they withdrew into the darkness again.

Drew couldn't help but smile. She was drawn up to her full height—little more than a child—and looked like a kitten with the fur standing up on its back.

"And if I had produced a knife?" he asked, his amusement growing.

She reached for her reticule, but before she could produce the pistol hidden there, he heard the unmistakable sound of two pistols being cocked. When his gaze returned to Lady Olivia, she had pointed a small pistol at his chest.

He raised his hands in defeat, and she smiled again, returning the pistol to its hiding place.

Offering her his arm, he said, "Would you care

to accompany me to a more comfortable spot where I can try and reason with you, and you can tell me to mind my own business? I think there is a secluded arbor with a bench close by. If we are the first to think of it, we should have it to ourselves. I would like to hear more of your tale."

A companionable silence fell as they walked to the small arbor. Drew was aware that Olivia's servants were following. They didn't speak, but their presence was palpable. It made the hair on the back of his neck stand on end, though he wasn't sure why. He felt certain that they knew he meant their mistress no harm and that they would not assault him without a command from her. Still, it was a peculiar feeling.

When Lady Olivia was seated on the bench, he stood over her, but she moved to one side, patting the small opening.

"I don't want you looming over me like some sort of vulture," she said.

Drew sat down, and he had to admit it was better sitting next to her. When she lifted her face to him, the moon's glow revealed every emotion, and her eyes sparkled like jewels.

"Now, what is this all about?" He resisted the urge to say "this foolishness," for he knew it would only annoy her.

"As you know, Lord Sheridan, I have a number of charities I support. Unlike some, however, I do more than give money. My school, for instance. I keep close tabs on how it is run, day to day. I visit it often."

"You go into the City, into the depths of the City, to this school?"

"It is perfectly safe. I have Harold to protect me. There is also Mr. Pate, my driver, and Rattle, my tiger. Nothing has ever occurred to make me reconsider."

"Speaking of Harold. He looks very familiar."

She chuckled and said, "Perhaps you know him from his days as a prizefighter?"

"That's it! Horrible Harry!" said the marquess.

"Yes, but he simply goes by Harold Hanson now."

"So you take Harold everywhere you go?"

"Yes, almost everywhere."

"And you think that makes it acceptable for you to go to these rather seedy neighborhoods?" asked the marquess.

"My visits to the school are not open for debate. I merely told you about them so that you will know that I take my charity work very seriously and very personally."

"I understand that, but it still does not explain why you would choose to stroll through the darkest, most dangerous pathways of Vauxhall."

"I was perfectly safe. Harold and Rattle are here."

"An overgrown . . ." He stopped, arrested by the look of warning in her eyes. He continued more temperately, "A large protector, perhaps, and a young man—hardly more than a boy. What would prevent someone from coming up behind them and knocking them senseless?"

"What nonsense! I suppose while this someone is attacking them, I will be standing there completely oblivious? That is not going to happen. I would scream, and then I would run away to get help for them."

"As I get to know you better, my dear Lady Olivia, I believe you would be more inclined to wade into the fray, both small fists flying."

She smiled at this, and he had the almost-overwhelming urge to take her into his arms again and taste those sweet lips once more. Some hint of this desire must have shown on his face, for Lady Olivia bowed her head. Whether she found it amusing that she held this power over him, he did not know, but the prospect gave him the strength to curb his lascivious impulse.

When she looked up again, her eyes pleaded for his understanding as she said, "I know it is not the wisest course of action, Lord Sheridan, but it is the only course open to me. I have long wanted to help these poor, unfortunate girls who, through the chance of birth, are doomed to live the life of prostitutes."

"My lady!" he mocked. "Such language!"

She squared her shoulders and said, "Neither the language nor the situation is acceptable, my lord, and I intend to do all I can to change this situation. Never think that I have deluded myself into thinking that I can help all of them, but if I can help a few, it is my . . ."

"Your passion does you credit, Lady Olivia, but there has to be a better way to go about it, a more efficient way, than putting yourself and your servants in harm's way."

"Perhaps you would be willing to . . ."

"No." Her face fell, and he wished he could make her smile again, but he didn't know how. Trying to explain, he said, "Coming to Vauxhall and hoping for a chance encounter with one of these ladies is not the answer. First of all, she may not want your help, like the one tonight. She may be perfectly satisfied with her situation."

"Nonsense! If you had not interrupted," she said, turning her face away from him.

"She was about to leave anyway, and you know it." He took her chin in his fingertips and turned her to face him again. "Admit it."

"Yes, I admit it," she said, her eyes now sparkling with tears that trickled down her cheeks like silver ribbons.

Drew fished in his pocket for a handkerchief and wiped her cheeks. At that moment, he would have done almost anything to make her smile again.

And then she did. Her eyes began to dance, and she clutched at his lapels, saying, "I have it! I know what we will do! There are places where one can find all sorts of these girls, all in one place. Brothels, I think they are called? Surely you know where these are, and you could take me there!"

He wrenched himself free and jumped to his feet, all the while shaking his head and holding up his hands to ward off such an improper suggestion. She was at his side, babbling.

She grew quiet when he took her by the shoulders and said firmly, "There is no way in this wide world, nothing in the power of the entire universe, that could make me agree to such a foolhardy scheme! Do not say another word about it!"

"But . . ."

He put up one hand to stop her.

"What is more, I want you to promise me that

you will not attempt such a ramshackle plan on your own." She shuffled her feet, and he added, "Promise, I say."

She heaved a sigh and hung her head. Mumbling, she said, "I promise."

"Good. Now, I don't know about you, but I have had my fill of Vauxhall for the night. Let me escort you to your carriage." She took the arm he offered, and they walked away.

When Drew had put her into her carriage, he leaned inside and said to the giant, "Her ladyship is to go straight home, is that understood?"

Harold looked to his mistress, who nodded. Then he nodded and said, "Very good, my lord."

Exhausted, Drew found his own carriage and headed home, too. He leaned against the soft squabs and thanked the heavens that he had been the one to discover Lady Olivia in the darkened pathways. It made his blood turn cold to think of what might have happened.

Now, however, he could rest easy. She had given him her word. She would not break it.

CHAPTER SIX

"Tonight was certainly a disaster," said Lady Olivia when the carriage was under way.

"I'm just glad it is over," muttered the big servant.

"Hardly over."

"But, m'lady, you promised."

"It is not over," said Olivia with a smug smile. "I never said I would not try to rescue them, Harold. I merely said that I would not do so alone. There is a difference."

"You don't mean you're going back to that Vauxhall place, do you, mistress?"

"No, I gave my word about that, but I have something else in mind. Don't worry. I am certain you will approve this time. It may take me a few days to put things in motion, but I shall come about."

"His lordship said . . ."

"Pish and tosh on his lordship. He has no power over me. And I do admit that perhaps I was going about things in the wrong way. I mean, how many nights could one spend at Vauxhall?" She was talking more to herself now than to her servant, but she was aware that he was listening intently.

"I have come to realize that I need help, and I think I know just the person to help me."

"Women," grumbled the marquess as his valet pulled off his coat. "I sometimes wonder how men and women manage to live in the same world. Women are such nonsensical creatures. I mean, you can never depend on them, can you, Fenwick?"

"No, my lord," said the valet, divesting his master of his waistcoat and then the cravat.

"And who can understand them? They give the impression of being these delicate flowers, but they are made of steel, I tell you. Do not be fooled by appearances."

"Certainly not, my lord," said Fenwick, holding out his master's dressing gown for him to put on. The valet stepped back when this was accomplished and waited patiently for further instructions.

"Lady Olivia, for instance. She gives the appearance of being an empty-headed, empty-hearted lady of Society—caring nothing for people, only for fashion—but there is a depth there that she doesn't show. She is quite an amazing lady."

"If you say so, my lord."

"Well, I do. Not to say that she is less maddening than other women. No, I would have to say that she is the most maddening of all the women I know."

Drew went to sit beside the fire and put his feet

up on a footstool. He picked up the book he was reading but didn't open it.

Behind him, his valet retrieved the bundle of discarded garments and waited. Finally, he said, "Will that be all, my lord?"

Drew waved a hand and said, "Yes, that's all. Good night, Fenwick."

"Good night, my lord."

When he was alone, Drew tried to erase the troubling evening from his mind. Suddenly, the logs cracked and sent a shower of sparks onto the hearth. His mind was drawn back to the arbor and Lady Olivia's sparkling eyes.

He should have kissed her again. There had been that moment—that hesitation. If he had taken her in his arms, he knew she would not have resisted. With a frown, he wondered if she would react the same with some other man.

No, that was unfair of him. Despite his musings about her spending the afternoon with Richard, he felt certain there was nothing between the two of them.

Still, it was not the first time she had been kissed. The thought made him get out of his comfortable chair and take the poker to stir the fire. Sparks flew, and again, he thought of Lady Olivia. There was fire beneath the empty-headed exterior she showed to Society. He certainly had been fooled.

With a frown, he returned to his chair. There was more than fire. There was compassion. Passion and compassion, a formidable combination. The sort of combination that might make a fellow forget the past and its pain.

"Hell and blast!" he muttered. "You, you old fool, need to get out of town for awhile."

Drew glared at the fire. He would be dashed if he left town because of some female!

Besides, he thought, who would see to it that she kept her promise? Her foolish generosity would land her in the suds, or worse. No, he had to stay close to keep an eye on her.

What Lady Olivia needed was a husband! That was it. Some kindhearted clunch who would fill her nursery with children.

Drew found he was grinding his teeth at this thought, but he ignored it. Instead, he tried to focus on that insipid smile she always had on her face at balls—the one that was permanently placed there despite how many country boobs stepped on her toes. And then there was her sweet consideration of others like that annoying chit Miss Featherstone. No, Lady Olivia might not be as shallow as he had at first thought, but her everlasting sunniness would drive him mad in a fortnight.

Yes, a husband was what Lady Olivia Cunningham needed, and he was the one to help her find one!

Olivia stroked the little cat's fur and looked out at the driving rain. She pulled her shawl more tightly about her shoulders and sighed.

"Wretched weather!" said Aunt Amy, entering the room and walking across to the windows to pull the drapes closed. "We should find something to do that will pass the time. What about a puzzle? Mr. Pendleton sent me a new one yesterday."

"He did?" said Olivia with a coy smile. "What

else has the good Mr. Pendleton sent to you?"

"Do not bother to tease me on that, my dear child. Mr. Pendleton sent me a puzzle because I mentioned that I enjoyed putting them together. He was just being kind."

"I see."

"No, you do not see. Heavens, Olivia, the man must be seventy! I know I am nearing the half-century mark, but I will not settle on just anyone. I am quite content to remain as I am, a companion to my spinster niece."

Their eyes met, and they burst into laughter.

Amy went to fetch her new puzzle, and when she returned, she poured out the pieces onto a table, and Olivia joined her there.

"What is it?" asked Olivia.

Holding the box, her aunt read, "It is called *Wallis's Royal Chronological Tables of English History.* Hm, so it is not a dissected map like the others I have. This should be quite amusing."

A silence descended on the duo as they concentrated on finding connecting pieces in the puzzle. After several minutes, Olivia noticed that her aunt's attention had wandered. She looked up to find her aunt staring at her intently.

"Yes?"

"Oh, nothing," said the older woman, picking up a piece of the puzzle and turning it over and over.

"Your attention is not being diverted by nothing, Aunt. What is it?"

"You are right, my dear. It was what I said a few minutes ago. About you being a spinster."

"I assure you, I did not take offense. After all, it is perfectly true."

Her aunt put down the piece and said, "But it need not be true. As a matter of fact, it *should not* be true. There is no reason for you to remain single. I know that I have voiced the opinion that it doesn't matter, and to some extent, that is true. For me, that is. Many years ago, I chose not to settle for second best."

"Did you?" asked Olivia, hoping to redirect her aunt's train of thought. "So you did turn down an offer that you sometimes regret."

"No, not at all. I do not regret it, not even now, after all these years."

"Who was it?" asked Olivia, hoping, after all these years that her curiosity would be satisfied, that she would finally learn why her aunt had chosen spinsterhood when she had had offers.

"It doesn't matter who it was. Suffice it to say, that for me, I could not accept a marriage where I would not come first. The young man had other things to accomplish in his life, and I was just an afterthought. That much was evident when he wed someone else not two months later."

"I am sorry, Aunt. Even though he was not worthy of you, it must have been a difficult decision for you."

"It was, but as I said, I still do not regret it."

Olivia asked quietly, "Did you love him so very much?"

When tears sprang to her aunt's eyes, Olivia jumped to her feet and circled the table, giving her aunt a quick embrace.

Aunt Amy shook her niece off and said gruffly, "I am not that distressed, my dear. After all, it was thirty years ago."

Suddenly, she gripped Olivia by the shoulders and said squarely, "Besides, we were speaking of you."

Olivia grinned and scampered around to her side of the table. "No, we were speaking of you. Do not trouble yourself with me, Aunt. I will marry if I decide I want to. Otherwise, I am quite content as I am. I have you, my friends, and my charities."

"Charities do not keep one warm at night."

"Blankets do," said Olivia. "Now, cheer up. This wretched weather has made both of us mope-eyed. Let's talk about other things. What gown are you wearing this evening? We must attend both the Winterses' musicale and Lady Osgood's rout, you know."

"Yes, and we shall be soaked before we get inside the first one. I would prefer to stay home, but I know Louisa Winters will have that son of hers singing, and he is so very talented. Sings like an angel."

"And looks like a bloodhound," said Olivia.

"Olivia! He does no such thing!" Her aunt's eyes started to twinkle, and she added, "Well, he does, but one mustn't say so, or it will be all I can do to sit and listen to him without laughing!"

They heard the front door open with a whoosh of wind. Amy said, "Now, who on earth could that be?"

"Someone very wet," whispered Olivia.

"And foolish," said her aunt.

The butler entered and inquired if they were at home to visitors. They nodded, and he threw open the door and announced, "Sir Richard Adair."

"Good afternoon, ladies. So good of you to see

me." He bowed over their hands and pulled up another chair to the table.

"Good afternoon, Sir Richard. Won't you join us?" said Olivia.

"I see you have found a way to amuse yourselves on this cold, wet day."

"We were just beginning. We can put it aside, if you prefer," said Aunt Amy.

"No, no, I would like to participate, if I may. I am so happy to be in company. I was like to be moped to death, sitting in my rooms."

"Then we are delighted you chose to visit us," said Olivia. "We were feeling much the same, weren't we, Aunt?"

"Indeed, yes. So glad you have called. I'm sure Witchell will come with a tea tray before long. You will join us, won't you?"

"Thank you, I would love that. Are you going to Lady Osgood's rout tonight?"

"Yes, one cannot allow the weather to hinder our little pleasures. Will you and the marquess be coming?" said Aunt Amy.

"Sheri? Heavens no! I'm afraid he is a bit displeased with me after I missed our rendezvous at Vauxhall last night."

"Oh, Vauxhall," said Aunt Amy. "I adore Vauxhall."

"Yes, but I simply forgot where I had asked him to meet me, never dreaming that we would not find one another. Anyway, when I saw him at the club earlier today, I asked if he was attending the rout, but he said that after that last one when Miss Featherstone fainted, he has sworn off them completely. Wouldn't even discuss the matter."

Olivia frowned at this. She had thought the handsome marquess might . . . not that she cared, though she had hoped to thank him for his concern the night before.

And for that kiss.

"Olivia, your mind is wandering. Sir Richard has asked what time we will be going."

"What? Oh, yes. Well, I am not certain. We plan to go to the Winterses' musicale first. Would you care to join us for that?"

"I hadn't planned to attend, but I might as well. Do you think you might grant me the honor of escorting you ladies?"

"Mind? It will be delightful to have a gentleman along," said her aunt.

He looked at Olivia with what she was sure he felt was a speaking look and asked, "And you, my lady? Do you have any objections?"

She managed not to laugh and replied, "Not at all, sir."

They turned as the door opened, and Witchell announced, "Lord Hardcastle, Miss Featherstone, and Miss Fallon."

The puzzle was forgotten. Minutes later, Witchell supervised the footman who carried a large silver tea tray into the drawing room. When the butler returned a moment later, he announced three more visitors, including Mr. Jenson.

"I say, this dreary afternoon is turning into a wonderful tea party," said Aunt Amy.

She moved to the middle of the sofa to allow Mr. Jenson room to join her and Miss Fallon.

"Witchell, more cups, if you please."

"I do hope you don't mind my dropping in,"

said Mr. Jenson. "I was coming to call on my patient, and I wouldn't have disturbed you, but I met the young people coming up the front steps, and . . ."

"You must never apologize for dropping in on us, Charles."

He almost dropped the tea cup she was handing him. Blushing, he stammered, "Thank you, Miss Hepplewhite."

"I used to be simply Amy," she said softly.

Glancing at her aunt, Olivia smiled, forgetting to pay attention to her conversation with Tony. Was it possible that Mr. Jenson was the young man from her aunt's past? It would explain a great deal about the way she had always treated the unfortunate doctor.

"Olivia, I asked you a question," said Lord Hardcastle.

"I am sorry, Tony. I was woolgathering, I'm afraid. What was it?"

"Nothing important. I only wanted to know when your two young people would be ready to go down to Castlebrook." When she frowned, he said, "The brother and sister who are going to work for me?"

"Oh, Martin and Winnie. Anytime would be fine. Only tell me when, and I will let Mrs. Priddy know. You know I truly appreciate this, don't you, Tony? They have only each other now and being together means the world to them. You are such a dear for taking both of them."

He smiled down at her and said, "You know I will always have a soft spot for you and your charitable proposals, Olivia. And Miss Featherstone feels much the same. She is such a sweet girl."

"I'm certain she is," murmured Olivia.

"Mr. Pendleton," announced Witchell.

Olivia watched as her aunt rose and went to greet the newcomer, leaving a frowning Mr. Jenson to his own devices.

"Will you excuse me a minute, Tony?"

"Certainly," he replied, and Olivia crossed the room to take her aunt's place on the sofa.

"Good afternoon, Mr. Jenson. How good of you to call on us. I know how busy you are," said Olivia.

"I . . . why, thank you, Lady Olivia. How is your maid doing?"

"It is little short of a miracle. I have never known anyone so sick to recover so quickly. It must have been your excellent medical care."

He smiled at this and shook his head but said, "Thank you." His eyes strayed to her aunt and he added, "I don't think everyone in this household thinks as highly of me as you do."

"Of course she does." Olivia covered her mouth with her fingertips and simpered, "I meant, of course we all do."

Forgetting the rest of the assemblage, the doctor took her hand and said, "If only I could believe she did feel like that about me." He dropped her hand and sighed. "I know it cannot be true. She has never forgiven me for . . . and truth be told, I have not much changed in all these years. I used to drive my wife to distraction—always missing my dinner, forgetting her birthday. I wasn't a very good husband."

Olivia patted his hand and said, "I am sure she did not think that. You mustn't be so hard on yourself, Mr. Jenson. And perhaps this time . . ."

"Lord Sheridan," said Witchell, causing Olivia to spring to her feet. She sat down immediately, then blushed a rosy pink.

"Is anything the matter?" asked her companion.

"What? Oh, no. I had, uh, forgotten something, but now I have remembered. I . . . it can wait. You were saying?"

From the threshold, Drew watched her unusual behavior with surprise. He had never seen the Lady Olivia be anything but unflappable in the social arena. The thought that his arrival might be the cause of this unnatural phenomenon made him want to turn and run. Instead, his dark glance swept the room, and he spied his friend Richard speaking to Pendleton and Miss Hepplewhite. They greeted him cordially when he joined them.

"It seems the entire world has gone mad, running around and visiting in this horrid weather."

"We are glad that you decided to join us, too, Lord Sheridan," said Miss Hepplewhite.

"As for me, I could not bear waiting for a break in the rain to leave my rooms," said Sir Richard. "I had already read the only book I own, and I refuse to play an old woman's game like patience."

"So he came here to help this old woman put together the wonderful puzzle you gave me, Mr. Pendleton," said Miss Hepplewhite. "It will have to wait, however, as we have all this amusing company to while away the afternoon."

"I have always thought that the company of like-minded people is by far the best way to spend one's time," said old Mr. Pendleton.

"And are we all like-minded?" asked Drew.

We'd Like to Invite You to Subscribe to Zebra's Regency Romance Book Club and Send You 4 Free Books as Your Introduction! (Worth $19.96!)

If you're a Regency lover, imagine the joy of getting 4 FREE Zebra Regency Romances and then the chance to have these lovely stories delivered to your home each month at the lowest price available! Well, that's our offer to you and here's how you benefit by becoming a Regency Romance subscriber:

- *4 FREE Introductory Regency Romances are delivered to your doorstep (you only pay for shipping & handling)*
- *4 BRAND NEW Regencies are then delivered each month (usually before they're available in bookstores)*
- *Subscribers save almost $4.00 off the cover price every month*
- *You also receive a FREE monthly newsletter, which features author profiles, discounts, subscriber benefits, book previews and more*
- *There's no risks or obligations...in other words, you can cancel whenever you wish with no questions asked*

Join the thousands of readers who enjoy the savings and convenience offered to Regency Romance subscribers. After your initial introductory shipment, you'll receive 4 brand-new Zebra Regency Romances each month to examine for 10 days. Then, if you decide to keep the books, you pay the preferred subscriber's price, plus shipping and handling.

It's a no-lose proposition, so return the FREE BOOK CERTIFICATE today!

Treat yourself to 4 FREE Regency Romances!
A $19.96 VALUE... FREE!
No obligation to buy anything ever!

lll..l..lll...ll.l.l.l..l..lll..l.l..l.l..lll..l

REGENCY ROMANCE BOOK CLUB

Zebra Home Subscription Service, Inc.

P.O. Box 5214

Clifton NJ 07015-5214

"Indeed we are. We are all alike in wanting to escape a dreary day all alone," said Pendleton.

"That is true enough," said Drew. "I think I will go and have a cup of tea."

"Yes, do. Olivia will pour for you."

Drew strolled over to the sofa, speaking to Lord Hardcastle on the way. When he stopped in front of Olivia, she smiled nervously.

"Good afternoon, Lady Olivia, Jenson. Might I trouble you for a cup of tea, Lady Olivia?"

"Here, let me move out of the way," said the doctor. "I should go and see my patient."

The doctor rose, leaving them alone in the gathering. The other guests chatted in clusters here and there, but no one paid any attention to the shaking hand that poured the tea or the smiling marquess.

"Has the weather given you a case of the megrims, my lady? Perhaps I should call the good doctor back to attend you," he teased.

This quip did not appear to amuse Lady Olivia in the least because she glared at him. Drew sipped the tepid liquid and watched her over the rim of the delicate cup.

After a moment, she smiled and said, "La, sir, I am quite well."

Her expression reminded him of the bird-witted Miss Fallon, and he wanted to shake her.

She heaved a sigh and breathed, "It is just that I am flustered by your handsome face. Your nearness makes my heart . . . ."

"A plumper if I ever heard one!" he hissed. All of a sudden, he smiled, and she responded in kind.

Leaning closer, he said, "Let us not allow things to become awkward between us, my lady. I know you are too kind a person not to forgive me for my boorish behavior last night, especially when I tell you that I know it was a mistake. What is more, I promise that it shall never happen again."

"I am glad to hear it. The more I thought about you telling me what I might or might not do, the more I realized how ridiculous it was. You have no power over me to tell me when and where I may practice my good works."

As she spoke, Drew's brows rose in astonishment, and he said, "What are you talking about?"

"Why, your boorish behavior, when you told me I couldn't go to Vauxhall anymore to . . . What were you talking about?" she demanded, her brows drawing together.

Her expression reminded him forcibly of the night before, in the arbor, when he had resisted the urge to take her into his arms again. It was out of the question now, though it would have stopped this foolish conversation.

Taking a deep breath to control his temper, he said, "I was talking about that blasted kiss. It should never have happened, and I apologize. And as I said a moment ago, I promise you it will never happen again!"

He waited while her emotions paraded across that expressive face. After a moment, she put in place that smile he so abhorred and said, "Do not worry, Lord Sheridan. I have no intention of ever letting that odious performance happen again. Now, if you will excuse me, I must consult with Mr. Jenson about the health of my maid. Good day."

She left the room. The rain had stopped and the sunlight, breaking through the clouds, gleamed into the elegant drawing room. The brightness, however, had fled with Lady Olivia, and the rest of the guests followed soon afterward.

As Richard bowed over Miss Hepplewhite's hand, he said, "What time this evening?"

"Nine o'clock. I am looking forward to it, Sir Richard."

"Me, too. Until nine."

Once they were on the street, Drew fell into step beside Richard, his mood a direct contrast with the sunlight.

"What's the matter, old chap?"

"What? Oh, nothing. I was only thinking of Lady Olivia."

"A delightful thought, no doubt."

"Delightful? Hardly that. The woman is enough to drive a man mad." At the gleam in his friend's eyes, Drew explained hastily, "Not that sort of mad. I mean truly mad. Do you know where I happened upon her last night?"

"I would say that wherever one happens upon such beauty is in itself a place of wonder and beauty, but I can see that such a poetic assertion would only get your back up. Therefore, I will simply ask, where?"

"At Vauxhall."

"Which is where I waited for you for at least an hour, but we shall return to that in a moment. Why is the fact that you met Lady Olivia at Vauxhall so unusual?"

"She was strolling, by herself, through the darkened pathways. At first, I thought she must be waiting for someone."

"An assignation? Hm, that alters my opinion of the good lady considerably," said Sir Richard.

"No, it was not like that at all. She was talking to a light skirt, trying to convince the creature that she should leave her profession and find a new life."

"As what?"

"I don't know, and neither does the girl, for she fled when I arrived. Anyway, Lady Olivia helps these sorts of girls learn a skill and gives them a place to live and so on. She said she has already had success with one or two. Have you ever heard anything so daft?"

"Daft? I would say it is admirable. And I will say again, that my opinion of the good lady was been altered—for the better. There is more there than meets the eye, though what meets the eye is quite lovely."

"Would you be serious for a moment?" said Drew.

"Very well. Behold me, completely serious. What did you do when you met her? I know what I would do if I were fortunate enough to meet that particular lady in a darkened lane, but I fear you are not as bold as I am."

"No, of course not," lied Drew, remembering those velvety lips on his. Shaking his head, he said, "I made her promise not to do such a dangerous thing ever again."

"And did she promise?"

"Yes, but quite reluctantly, and just a moment ago, she was going on and on about it, as though she had never made such a promise. She said I had no right to demand such a promise of her. . . ."

"As you do not, because you are not related to the lady," said his friend.

"I know, and I am afraid that she will try again. To make matters worse, she mentioned last night that she could have more success in this venture if she could find someone to take her to a brothel where she could meet them all together."

Sir Richard's booming laughter caused passersby to stare, but he didn't seem to care.

Clutching at Drew's sleeve, he regained control of himself and said, "And are you going to help? I am certain you know of one or two likely places."

"That is what Lady Olivia said," grumbled Drew. "She wanted me to take her . . . me!"

The absurdity of this suddenly hit him full force, and his own laughter spilled forth. For a moment, the two gentlemen found it impossible to continue their stroll until they had had their fill.

Still gasping, Richard said, "You know, Drew, it really is an admirable sentiment."

"Perhaps, but I think it is born out of misplaced sentiment. If Lady Olivia had a husband to keep her occupied and preferably several children in her nursery, she would not get involved in such a harebrained scheme," said Drew.

His friend stopped and stared. "Are you telling me that you are going to take the post?"

"Me? Now you are dicked in the nob! I would no more wed the lady than . . . I would wed you! The last thing I have ever wanted was another wife, especially one like the last one! What would I want with another who is so tied up with London Society? No, I intend to help the lady find a husband. I will be doing a service to both Lady Olivia and the rest of unsuspecting London." Drew continued along the pavement.

Following after his friend, Sir Richard said, "A husband for Lady Olivia, eh?"

Drew stopped in his tracks. Though he gave his companion a sharp look, he said nothing. Whistling, Sir Richard walked away.

Drew caught up to him in a few steps and said, "Richard, what were you talking about with Miss Hepplewhite when we were leaving?"

"Talking about?"

"You know. Nine o'clock and all."

"Oh, that. I was just setting the time that I should arrive to escort them on their round of entertainments this evening."

"You are serving as escort?"

"Yes, I happened to arrive first this afternoon and asked if they were attending Lady Osgood's rout—which you vowed to avoid, you will remember. Anyway, they said that they were going, but only after the Winterses' musicale. Because I couldn't be certain what time to meet up with them at the rout, they suggested I simply accompany them to both."

"Who suggested it? Lady Olivia or Miss Hepplewhite?"

"I don't . . . now that you ask, I think it was Lady Olivia. Hm, interesting, don't you think?"

Drew had never wanted so much to plant his friend a facer. Instead, he said, "You are not thinking of . . . that is, when I was speaking of finding a husband to occupy Olivia's time, I was not thinking of you."

"Neither was I, dear chap," said the rake. "On the other hand, neither of us has a crystal ball to see into the future, do we? I suppose only time will tell."

CHAPTER SEVEN

Sir Richard presented himself promptly at nine o'clock. He wore a black coat and black pantaloons. His cravat was tied in the intricate mathematical. His only jewelry was a gold signet ring and a ruby stickpin. His handsome face was crowned by dark hair, brushed very carefully into a careless windswept style. He was the epitome of the English gentleman, and his elegant appearance did not stir Olivia's heart one iota.

"Good evening, ladies. You are looking especially fetching this evening. I shall be the envy of all the other gentlemen when I appear with two such dazzlers on my arms."

"La, sir, you will turn our heads," said Olivia.

"Pray continue," said her aunt, giggling like a schoolgirl.

"That color of lavender is quite becoming on you, Miss Hepplewhite. You look the veriest girl in it."

"That's good enough. I will not look nearly as

young with your butter boat turned over my head.
Let us be on our way," said Aunt Amy.

Their first stop was the Winterses' musicale. It
was a small affair with only thirty or forty guests.
Sir Richard found them seats across from the small
platform Lady Winters had had erected for the
performers. The first performer was a young lady
who played the harp remarkably well.

"A wonderful performance," said Sir Richard.

"And seemingly so effortless. I do so admire anyone with musical talent," said Olivia.

"Well, I never would have guessed," murmured
her aunt, her attention suddenly drifting.

Olivia turned to see who or what had diverted
her aunt. She smiled and gave a little wave to Mr.
Jenson as he entered the room. Weaving behind
the scattered chairs of the audience, he reached
their side.

"Good evening, ladies, Sir Richard," he whispered.

"Do you not realize it is rude to enter when
someone is in the middle of her performance?"

Olivia's mouth fell open at this, and the doctor
blushed.

"I am sorry, Lady Winters told me to come right
in."

"You should have taken that empty seat by the
door," said Aunt Amy.

Her three listeners squirmed in their seats, but
even Olivia could not think of a way to curb her
aunt's tongue.

The doctor stammered and then said firmly, "I
will leave if you wish, Miss Hepplewhite. My thought

in coming over was to have the pleasure of sitting with friends, with you, in particular, but if you find my presence so distasteful, I will certainly leave."

"I did not say your company was distasteful, Mr. Jenson. Did you hear me say that, Olivia?" asked Aunt Amy.

Just then, the young lady on stage finished her piece.

Before she could begin her second offering, Sir Richard said, "I think I shall go and fetch all of us something cool to drink."

"I will go with you, Sir Richard," said Olivia, rising and taking his arm.

"That was certainly uncomfortable," he remarked as they reached the dining room where a buffet of light refreshments was displayed.

"I have never heard my aunt be so incredibly rude."

"It must be love," he said, picking up a cup and filling it with champagne punch.

Accepting the cup, Olivia said, "You have a very low opinion of love, Sir Richard, if you think it can so easily take on the guise of rudeness."

"No, I am merely being truthful. In my experience, love makes a person behave quite strangely. Do you not agree? I mean, when you fancy yourself in love, do you not have palpitations and find yourself in alt one moment and in the depths of despair the next?"

"I couldn't say. I have never been in love," she replied quietly.

His look of astonishment was worthy of the stage, and he said, "I would never presume to call a lady a liar, but I find your confession impossible to believe. A beauty like you, never in love? *Incroyable!* I simply cannot believe it."

"Nonetheless, it is true."

"Does this mean," he said, grabbing his throat dramatically, "that you are not in love with me? Not just a little? Be careful how you answer, my lady, for I warn you, I may have to put period to my existence if you deny it."

Olivia giggled but put her finger to her lips as another couple entered the room. They greeted them politely and strolled to the other side of the table.

Clutching at her elbow, Sir Richard said, "I await your response, but before you reply, my dear Lady Olivia, I beg you to recognize that you hold my life—nay, my very soul—in the palm of your hand."

"You, my dear Sir Richard, are the most absurd man I have ever met."

His hand to his heart now, he said, "Ah, she has called me her 'dear.' I cannot hope for more. Come, we must join the others before you take back the boon you have so generously bestowed on me."

They returned to the drawing room where the young harpist was standing and receiving her just applause.

Olivia took one look at her stiff-necked aunt and groaned. How awkward it was going to be if she did not get over whatever had caused her to be so rude to the doctor. For his part, the doctor now seemed as angry as her aunt did.

Several more performers, mostly mediocre, took their turns on the stage. Finally, it was time for Lady Winters's son to take the stage. A lad of fourteen, he had been performing for his mother's friends since the age of six. He had dark brown hair and deep-set eyes, rather like a bloodhound's.

Aunt Amy leaned over and whispered, "He is much improved in appearance. His head has finally grown to his nose."

"Shh!" hissed Olivia, stifling a laugh.

Master Winters opened his mouth to sing. The first few notes were angelic. Then his voice squeaked, and the warbling melody fell an entire octave. After the first few seconds of the poor boy's performance, a number of the guests seemed to require refreshments and sought refuge in the other room. Olivia and Sir Richard, along with a fuming doctor and aunt, stayed until the bitter end. Somehow, Olivia managed to keep her social smile intact.

The doctor excused himself after the musicale, saying that he had patients to check on. Aunt Amy refused to even look at the poor man.

Sir Richard escorted the ladies to the Osgood rout. It was a terrible crush, and conversation among the three of them proved impossible.

By the time they had managed to regain the street, Aunt Amy was in such a state that they went straight home. When they arrived, she seemed to perk up, and Sir Richard was persuaded to join them for tea.

Witchell soon brought in the tray, and Aunt Amy busied herself with pouring while Richard entertained them with the latest *on-dit* from his club.

"Tell me," said Aunt Amy. "Are the wagers placed at the tables so ruinous?"

"Occasionally. I do not indulge in that myself," he replied.

"Too virtuous?" teased Olivia.

"Too poor. Well, too poor compared with some of the members. Besides, unlike my friend Sheri, I am a lover, not a gambler."

"So you prefer the ladies to cards?" asked Aunt Amy. When he nodded, she added, "Isn't that lucky for us, Olivia? Otherwise we would have been quite without an escort tonight. So much more pleasant the way it turned out."

"Does Lord Sheridan gamble so much?" asked Olivia, carefully keeping her tone careless. She had nothing against gambling, but there were so many better ways to spend one's money.

"No, not really. He likes a hand of cards or two. I sometimes wonder why Sheri even belongs to the club, except that it is what we gentlemen do." The clock on the mantle chimed the hour, and he rose. "That, and keep lovely ladies up much too late with our frivolous chatter. It has been a great pleasure, ladies, but I must bid you good night."

When he had gone, the ladies expelled little sighs of relief. It had been a very long day.

Heaving another sigh, Aunt Amy said, "That Sir Richard is quite the charmer."

"I suppose so. And wasn't it nice of Mr. Jenson to come?" said Olivia, sinking back against the sofa in the drawing room and kicking off her kid slippers.

"He probably had to find something to occupy his time between seeing patients. I much prefer someone like your Sir Richard, someone you can count on."

"He is not *my* Sir Richard, Aunt, but he is certainly obliging. I don't know many men who would accompany two ladies to two such boring parties. The musicale would have been fine, I suppose, if young Master Winters's voice had not decided to change this very evening. How mortifying for the lad."

"His mother should have dragged him off the stage after the first chorus. I always doubted her good sense, and now I am sure of it."

"Aunt, do not be so hard on her. She is just a doting mother."

"Well, your mother was doting, too, but when she realized you had the ear of a rock, she let you quit your music lessons—of any kind."

Olivia giggled. "Yes, but not before having me try everything from the pianoforte to the harp. The worst, however, was the lute. She told me I had an old-fashioned voice and needed to play an appropriate instrument."

"Oh, I remember that. I came running down the stairs, accusing the potboy of strangling that cat you had."

"What I really needed was something very loud to drown out my voice. Unfortunately, there is no instrument a young lady can play that would be that loud."

"That's all right, m'dear. You have a kind heart and that is better than musical talent any day." Her aunt rose and stretched. "I am going to bed. I am supposed to have a fitting for my new gown at eleven o'clock, but I daresay I shall have to cancel it. Somehow, as I get older, morning comes earlier. Good night, my dear."

"Good night, Aunt. Sleep well."

When Olivia was alone, she lifted the hem of

her gown and put her feet out to the fire. *Would winter never give up?* she wondered. She shivered and leaned forward to warm her hands.

Olivia smiled, remembering some of the outrageous compliments Sir Richard had paid her. He really was a charming man. She had not believed any of his flummery, and he, she could tell, knew it. Still, they had enjoyed their nonsense. His was such a charismatic personality. A shame his friend was not gifted in that way.

She grimaced at the sofa, the empty spot by her side where the marquess had sat that very afternoon. Why had he felt compelled to say all those awful things? For a man to kiss a woman without permission was not polite, but for him to claim it had meant nothing, that it had been a mistake—that was near to heresy!

And she had thought the marquess possessed a modicum of good sense!

What made matters worse, she must be as much of a nincompoop as he was—else why would his words have wounded her so?

Closing her eyes, she relived that kiss, every mind-numbing second of it. She could feel his arms around her, the silky feel of his hair.

Becoming uncomfortable, Olivia shifted away from the fire. How had it grown so warm? Returning to her memories, she groaned.

She had been so foolish! She should never have responded to him. At first, she had been quite shocked—not by the kiss so much as by the fact that it was the cynical marquess delivering it—and to her, whom he barely tolerated. But it was not as if she had never been kissed. She had, but she had never been tempted to respond as . . . feverishly as she had last night. In retrospect, her response had been quite scandalous. She could not, in good conscience, however, bring herself to regret it for it had opened the floodgate for that delicious, overwhelming feeling of . . .

Olivia frowned. What had she felt when he had continued kissing her in that wonderful manner? When had he begun to probe her mouth, and for that matter, when and why had she allowed it? The warmth that had flooded her body had been equally astonishing.

She found her breath was coming rapidly just remembering his touch, the scent of him in the crisp night. She closed her eyes, imagining he was there, that she was in his arms.

Olivia's eyes flew open, and she gasped.

Desire.

She had felt wild and inescapable desire.

She clambered to her feet, still reeling from this realization. Taking a turn around the room, she came back to the fire, staring into it until her heart quit thumping so loudly.

He was right. He should never have kissed her. If he had never kissed her, then she would not know this wrenching feeling of emptiness, knowing that he never intended to kiss her again.

She clenched her fists. "Damn you," she whispered. The curse did nothing to alleviate her desolation.

"What I should do," she told the fire, "is to find the most disagreeable female in all of London and make you fall in love with her and marry her. That would fix you, my Lord Sheridan."

This thought brought with it a pain as real as if someone were stabbing her with a knife. She uttered a small, frustrated cry and clutched the mantle for support.

There would be no finding a wife for the marquess now. Olivia lifted her chin and looked into the small mirror over the fireplace. No, there was no need to search.

She had discovered the perfect mate for Lord Sheridan.

And he would never know.

Morning, as always, restored Olivia's cheery mood. When she rose and looked out the window at the new, gleaming day, she could not prevent the burst of hope that flamed in her breast.

Having never felt the sting of Cupid's arrow, she had never pursued a man before. Now, she would have to learn, and she would have to learn fast. It was the first of May already. The Season would be over before she knew it, and with it, her chances to make the marquess realize that she was the one he needed in his life, the one who could make him smile.

The clock chimed ten, and she put on her wrapper and tripped down the hall to her aunt's room. Her aunt sat in the bed, her bed cap askew, sipping her morning chocolate.

"Good morning, my dear."

"You are up very early," said Olivia, crossing the room and sitting on the side of the bed.

"Yes, well, Jinks reminded me last night that if I did not have my fitting today, my gown would probably not be ready for our ball in two weeks' time. Because I simply must have a new gown for that, I told her to wake me even if I threw every single pillow at her head."

"Which she did," said the maid, coming into the room, her arms laden with all manner of petticoats, stockings, and a navy blue carriage dress.

"Yes, yes, and I shall have something to say about that at some later date, but for now, please, Jinks, do take that dress away. You know I cannot abide wearing it in May. May calls for pale lilacs and soft greens. Don't you agree, my dear?"

"Oh, yes. In May, one shouldn't wear navy blue unless one is in mourning."

"There, you see, Jinks! I am not alone in my opinion. Bring me the pale green. It always makes me feel like a girl again."

"Speaking of feeling like a girl, Aunt, what did you say to Mr. Jenson yesterday to fluster him so?"

"Say? Why, nothing. What should I have said? The man is a ninny. Do you know, when I told him that we would be going to both the Osgood's rout and the Winterses' musicale, he said he did not know if he could attend? Something about patients again. I was completely put out with the man and still am."

Aunt Amy took refuge in a long sip of her chocolate, but her pale blue eyes were fierce, daring Olivia to argue with her.

Raising her delicate brows, Olivia said, "And you certainly let him know when he came to the Winters' musicale."

"He deserved no better," said her aunt.

"I can see how you might be upset, Aunt, but

did it never occur to you that Mr. Jenson might not have received invitations to the musicale or the rout? He is from a good family, but he has not cultivated Society through the years because of his medical work. It is possible he does not even know either family."

"As if I would not smooth things over with both Lady Winters and Lady Osgood," she sniffed. "Still, I had not thought of that."

"Yes, and by telling him about it like you did, he probably thought you were simply pointing out the fact that he does not travel in the same lofty circles as you and I."

"I never! Oh, dear, yes. I can see where Charles might think that exactly. As I said, he is a complete ninny," she added, but her tone was tender.

Her aunt climbed out of bed and strode to the small secretary that stood on the far side of the room.

"I shall have to remedy this," she said, sitting down. After pulling out paper and pen, she hesitated, her shoulders sagging.

Turning back to Olivia, she said, "If I write to him, there is no way to guarantee that he will even respond."

"What if Pansy took a turn for the worse?"

"Do you think she might?" asked her aunt.

"If we asked her to," laughed Olivia.

"No, no, he would see through that in a minute. He is, after all, an excellent physician. And though I do not wish for him to think I was boasting about our social standing, I still would not like for him to think that I was so desperate for his company that I would lie about Pansy's health."

"But you are that desperate, are you not?" asked Olivia.

Her aunt expelled a girlish giggle and nodded. "Olivia, I'm afraid I am smelling of April and May, but I have no clue about him, you know. There was a time, years ago, when he professed to love me."

"He does seem to show up on our doorstep with amazing regularity."

"Yes, but that is often because someone is ill." Her aunt crossed the room and plopped down on the bed beside her. "Am I only being a foolish old woman?"

"I cannot think of two less likely words to use to describe you, my dear aunt." She put her arm around her aunt's shoulder and squeezed. Hopping off the bed, she added, "Whatever we decide, we must get going if you are to make it to your fitting on time. The ladies have been working hard, I know, for they gave me a peek the other day. As for me, I have decided to have a new gown for the ball as well."

"Oh, it is a special occasion. But I thought you said the maroon one would do."

"Yes, and so it would, but now I think I would prefer to wear blue. I saw the most beautiful cloth at Layton and Shears. We can stop there first and then proceed to the widows' home for your fitting."

"It was not a navy blue," warned her aunt.

"No, a beautiful sky blue, sparkling with silver threads," said Olivia, dreaming of the marquess's reaction upon seeing her in such a gown.

"We must be careful, my girl." Olivia raised her brows and her aunt added, "Lest we make all of London fall in love with us."

* * *

"What have you got there?" asked Richard, peering across the narrow table where Drew was writing.

"A list of men for Lady Olivia. I have let my idea slide, but I think it is time to put it into action."

Richard picked up the paper and scanned it, chuckling as he handed it back. "Pendleton? You cannot be serious! The man is an ancient. The difference in age is too immeasurable. It would be like Methuselah wedding a schoolgirl."

"There have been similar marriages," grumbled the marquess.

"Perhaps, but you don't seriously think Lady Olivia would ever agree to such a farce."

"Not really. I had Hardcastle on there, but he is taken. He would be the most likely candidate if it weren't for Miss Featherstone."

"Hardly, he and Lady Olivia are more like brother and sister. Rumor has it that she turned him down years ago."

"I didn't know that. Very well, then there is your cousin, Thomas."

"Not the marrying sort, my cousin. Now Campion, there's a paper skull for you. Even if he could somehow be transformed into an acceptable suitor, she would run circles about the lad."

"He is not so bad. He received the highest marks at school."

"Which he only just left." Holding out his hand, Richard said, "Here, hand me the pen and paper."

He wrote for several minutes, holding his hand across the top of the paper to keep Drew from seeing what he was writing. Finally, with a flourish, he handed it to the marquess.

"Here is a real list. Make what you will of that."

"Palmer? Good God, man. Palmer's interested in nothing but politics, and he has voted against every measure that would give relief to the poor. And Brady? All he cares about is snuff." Drew slashed the names from the list and glared at his friend.

"There are others. Keep reading."

"Not Adler! You cannot be serious about Adler. The man is a womanizer and a pervert. And Vincent prefers boys to girls."

"Then cross them off. There are several others."

Muttering, Drew continued to read, wielding his pen after each name. "Foster—too poor. Carstairs—too annoying."

At the end, he looked up at his friend. Richard grinned and shrugged. Drew carefully crossed out the final name.

"Not fair, old boy," Richard complained. "I don't give a fig about politics. I do not indulge in snuff. I prefer girls to boys, and though I am not as rich as you, I do have sufficient funds. What's more, Lady Olivia likes me. She doesn't find me in the least annoying."

"And what about womanizing? I notice you did not compare yourself with Adler."

"True, but he is a pervert, and I am not. Nor am I a saint, but then I do not think Lady Olivia requires a saint."

"She won't have you."

"Perhaps not, but I intend to have a run at it."

"She is not an it," mumbled the marquess.

"No, she is a lovely young lady. We spent last night laughing and chatting. I cannot imagine a more pleasant type of wife."

"I thought you planned never to marry."

"Plans are made to be broken. Now, let us lay all this aside. Lady Olivia and her charming aunt are going to be at the Featherstones' ball tonight. Lord Featherstone will be announcing the betrothal of his daughter to Hardcastle. Lady Olivia has promised me the first waltz."

"I will be along later," said Drew. He sat back in his chair, crossing his ankles to indicate that he was in no hurry.

"Very well, suit yourself. I hope to see you there."

Richard left the room, and Drew muttered, "Oh, you will most assuredly see me there. I wouldn't miss it for the world."

Olivia patted her hair as she and her aunt went up the stairs and into the Featherstone ballroom. She felt a little shiver of excitement as she looked over the dancers.

"May I hope that smile is for me, Lady Olivia?" asked Sir Richard, arriving at her side. He offered an arm to each lady and led them into the room.

"I was certainly smiling in your direction, Sir Richard," she replied.

"If you two are going to spend the evening making inane conversation again, I will leave you to it and find some sensible company," said Aunt Amy. With a regal nod to them both, she left them to seek her friends.

Bending close to Olivia's ear, he whispered, "I thought she would never leave."

"That is too bad of you, Sir Richard," replied Olivia with a trill of laughter.

"I cannot help being bad when you are at my side. You look marvelous tonight by the way."

"Thank you, sir. Have you come to claim your dance?" asked Olivia.

"Not a mere dance, my dear lady. A waltz. You promised me the first waltz."

"Are you certain? I don't recall any stipulations," she lied.

"I am wounded that you could forget. But I shall forgive you, on one condition."

"And what is that, Sir Richard?"

"That you also save the supper dance for me."

"Alas, it is already promised."

"To whom?" he demanded, looking this way and that as if to spy the culprit.

"I cannot say, but I have a previous claim on that particular boon."

"I am desolate, of course, but listen. The musicians are striking up the next dance, and unless my ears deceive me, it is to be a waltz. Shall we?" he said, offering his arm.

Olivia took his arm and was swept onto the floor. Sir Richard was a graceful man, and she had no trouble following his lead. Being so adept at it, she also had no need to concentrate on avoiding his feet.

If he were only someone else, someone with dark eyes and dark hair. Her smile became dreamy as she imagined she was waltzing in Lord Sheridan's arms.

As if she had conjured him, he appeared at the top of the stairs, watching them, staring at them. She missed a step when she realized he did not have his cane.

"What is it, my dear?" asked Sir Richard, his gaze following hers. "Ah, so that is what has taken your thoughts away from me."

"Not at all," she simpered, gazing up at him with what she hoped were soulful eyes. "It is simply that Lord Sheridan doesn't have his cane with him."

"Hm, I wonder what can have possessed him. Well, never mind. You are mine for the moment, and I shall simply have to redouble my efforts. Your eyes are as blue as the Mediterranean Sea. A fellow could get lost . . . in . . . those . . . oh, what's the use. Stare to your heart's content, m'dear. No one will notice."

She took her eyes off the handsome marquess long enough to smile at Sir Richard. They continued their waltz in silence. She was aware that Sir Richard, gentleman that he was, tried to turn so that she would have the best view of his friend.

When the dance was over and she thanked Sir Richard, he took her hand and lifted it to his lips.

"I wish you the best of luck, my lady. You will need it where my rather dense friend is concerned. Here he comes now. Best to act casual," said Sir Richard, winking at her before extending his hand to the marquess.

"Good evening, old chap."

"Evening," said the marquess, his eyes on Olivia.

She tried to keep her color even as she replied, "Good evening, Lord Sheridan. Where is your cane?"

"Cane? I have decided to change my spots." He cocked his head to one side and smiled.

Olivia felt her face turning pink, and she coughed to cover her discomfiture.

"Demmed strange thing to do, all of the sudden," said Sir Richard. "You once said you would forgo it if something or other froze over."

"Actually, it was something your aunt said to me, Lady Olivia. I cannot recall our conversation precisely, but it made me think that I have become too predictable. I thought I would see what it is that brings rogues like Richard here to this sort of affair."

"You intend to dance?" said his friend.

Now it was the marquess's turn to blush, and he demurred, "I . . . I hadn't gotten that far in my thinking."

"So you do not intend to dance?" asked Olivia in a small voice. Her blush deepened. She had practically asked the man to dance!

The marquess felt the strain of their conversation, too, because he hedged, "That, uh, remains to be seen."

"Good evening, gentlemen." Lord Hardcastle bowed before them and asked, "Lady Olivia, may I have the pleasure of the next dance?"

"Yes, please, Tony," she said with obvious relief.

The marquess scowled, and she relaxed. Things were back to normal. She looked up at her childhood friend and giggled. Lord Sheridan glared at his friend and then stalked away. Though Olivia listened to Tony's conversation and responded as needed, she watched the marquess as he went to sit with her aunt.

* * *

"Why the deuce are you looking so out of sorts, my lord?" asked Miss Hepplewhite. She edged her chair closer to his, blocking her other cronies from listening to their conversation.

He sat uneasily without his cane to fiddle with or lean on. He hardly knew what to do with his hands. Finally, he crossed his arms.

It was obvious to Drew that Miss Hepplewhite was having trouble controlling her amusement, and she said, "Now that you have that settled, Sheri, whatever is the matter?"

"Nothing." When she raised a brow at this, he said, "Everything."

He looked into those faded blue eyes and realized suddenly that he could not confide his matchmaking plans to Miss Hepplewhite. She probably didn't know about Olivia's foolish attempts to rescue light skirts, and it would only worry her. And without that information, she would not understand why he wanted to find Lady Olivia a suitable husband to curb her philanthropic endeavors.

Somehow, he had envisioned coming to the ball, dancing once with Olivia and then, with the help of her aunt, seeing to it that for the rest of the evening, Olivia's partners should all be eligible suitors.

But Olivia was no fool, and she would not welcome his interference. What was more, if he danced with her and only with her, then everyone would assume . . . Drew shuddered.

"If you are not going to tell me, Lord Sheridan, then there is nothing I can do to help," said Amy.

Unfolding his arms, he patted her hand and

said, "I find that I cannot confide in you after all, Amy." This was delivered in quiet, intimate tones that caused the older woman's color to rise.

"Suffice it to say, your niece needs a husband. I want to help her find one."

Amy frowned. After a moment, she whispered, "Do you mean that you are not in the running for the job, but you would like to help find someone suitable?"

He nodded, and the older woman chortled, holding her sides, she was laughing so hard. People were beginning to stare, and Drew pounded her back, pretending she was choking.

Amy regained her senses and stopped. Thanking him for his "aid," she whispered, "I wish you much luck, my dear Sheri, but I fear your efforts are doomed. My niece, I believe, plans to remain a spinster, just like her foolish old aunt."

"But why?"

"You must ask her that yourself. I don't know. I have warned her that she may have left it too late, but she will not listen. She insists she is content as she is. I have told her that spinsterhood is a very lonely state. If I had known years ago what it would be like, I might have done things differently, but I was proud, perhaps too proud. And now it is too late."

"Miss Hepplewhite, may I have the honor of the next dance?"

Drew and Amy sprang apart like guilty children. Drew rose to greet Mr. Jenson. When the formalities were accomplished, the doctor repeated his request.

Amy Hepplewhite lifted her chin and said, "Certainly not, you old fool. As if I would make a spectacle of myself at this ball, in front of all my friends."

The doctor's hopeful expression fell, and he turned away.

Drew stopped him. "Mr. Jenson, you may have my seat. I am in need of refreshments. I am certain Miss Hepplewhite would welcome someone sensible to talk to, even though she does not dance."

"Oh. Oh!" said the doctor, understanding making him smile again. "May I sit with you, Miss Hepplewhite?"

"There is nothing to stop you, I suppose," she replied, her tone haughty but not as cold as before. Before Drew could walk away, she added, "I do wish you luck, Lord Sheridan."

"Thank you, Miss Hepplewhite."

Drew wandered along the edge of the ballroom, in search of something strong to fortify him. He found it in the card room and leaned against the wall to study the play.

His friend Lady Thorpe entered and joined him. Before he knew it, he was confiding in her, telling her an abbreviated version of his encounter with Lady Olivia at Vauxhall and his subsequent plan to find her a husband.

Maddie chuckled at this and said, "And how do you plan to accomplish this? I know that Lady Olivia has been on the Town for a number of Seasons, and she has yet to accept an offer. What makes you think you can come up with someone who will change her mind?"

"You're right, but I must do something."

"Then marry her yourself," said Lady Thorpe.

"Maddie, you must be mad. You know I don't want a wife, and I am the last person she would accept. No, there has to be someone ... someone worthy and yet, exciting. Someone new. Surely with all the officers who served against Napoleon coming home, there will be someone new."

"You are not speaking of Richard, I hope. He is hardly marriage material for one such as Lady Olivia."

"No, no. I had not considered him. Although, they seem to be getting along very well, but I fear Richard is only after a bit of dalliance."

"Very probably. He is not worth anything else."

Drew shot her an inquiring glance, but she ignored it. A moment later, he snapped his fingers and said, "I have it. Is there anyone who has come home wounded? Not too badly, just enough to make him interesting to a female who likes fixing things."

"Perhaps you should place an advertisement in the *Post*," she quipped.

"No, but I shall ask Richard."

"If Richard is busy trying to seduce the lovely Olivia, then it is unlikely that he will want to help you find a suitably impaired suitor," observed Maddie.

"True, I hadn't thought of that." Drew mulled this over for a moment and then said, "He need not know why I want to locate such a man. I shall tell him I need someone, a career officer whose injuries have forced him to retire, to help with my charities."

"That might entice him," she said doubtfully.

"Yes, and for now, I shall question Lady Olivia

about her willingness to give such a gentleman a chance. I think I know the answer," he said as they strolled into the ballroom. He spied his quarry among the dancers and grimaced. She was laughing at something her partner said, enjoying herself immensely.

"Perhaps I should look for someone who is still fit enough to haul himself about the dance floor."

"Speaking of that, where is your cane? I nearly fell over when I realized you had not brought one."

"I had thought to dance," he said.

"With me?" she asked. "How kind of you, Sheri."

"Maddie, I . . . well, why not. I certainly won't mind dancing with you," he grumbled.

"You are too kind," she murmured. "Your flattery is going to turn my head, Lord Sheridan."

"All right. Will you honor me with the next dance, my dear Lady Thorpe?"

"I would be delighted," she replied, taking his arm.

The dance was a quadrille. Drew found he was having to concentrate on the steps. He had danced so seldom in the past few years. As he watched the other gentlemen in his square and followed their lead, he realized how foolish he would have looked to have attempted dancing with Lady Olivia. And the waltz, the only time he had tried that had been the past Christmas when Rebekah had plagued him so to practice with her.

Maddie was good company, he thought, as he parted from her again. She never asked foolish questions. Her conversation was as rational as any man's. It was a shame that her marriage had been unhappy. He could have predicted it. Thorpe had had a reputation as a depraved man. She should have wed Richard, but he had been hot to join a regiment and see some action. Poor Maddie. Still, now that she was a widow, she seemed quite content.

When the steps of the dance brought them together again, he asked impulsively, "Are you happy, Maddie?"

"Happy? Why do you ask me that, Sheri?"

"It occurred to me that you might not be, and I would want to help, if I could."

"I am quite . . . content, and I think contentment is all I need for the moment."

"So widowhood is satisfactory."

She giggled and pressed his hand. "If you think you are going to help me find a husband, you are wide of the mark, Sheri. I have said it before, and I will say it again. Nothing could make me wed again. Surely you, of all people, can understand that. You feel much the same, do you not?"

"Yes, yes, of course I do."

"Then please believe me when I say that I am quite content to remain unwed. I will let you know, however, if that should change. Perhaps you should go into the business of matchmaking. Hang out a shingle."

The steps separated them again, and Drew gladly let the subject fall. Why was he suddenly so obsessed with marriage? He shuddered and reminded himself that it was only Lady Olivia's marriage state that bothered him. From now on, he would concentrate on her and her alone.

The music drew to a close. Everyone stopped as

the musicians played a fanfare. Lord Featherstone was standing on the small dais, slightly elevated above the guests.

"Before we have the musicians play the supper dance—a waltz, by the way, we have an announcement to make." He signaled his daughter and Lord Hardcastle to join him.

"We are pleased to announce the betrothal of our dear daughter Fanny to Lord Hardcastle. Please, join me in a toast."

The footmen had been busily circulating with trays of glasses, and after a glance around the room, Lord Featherstone said, "To the happy couple!"

"To the happy couple!" seconded everyone in the crowd.

"Now, back to the festivities."

The musicians played a short introduction to the melody while the guests found their partners.

Drew opened his mouth to speak to Maddie and found Lady Olivia had appeared at his side in her place.

Quickly recovering from the surprise, he said, "My lady, you do not dance?"

"I fear I have not been asked for this particular set," she said, casting her blue eyes to the ground as she sighed.

"Would you do me the honor?" he asked, noticing that his mouth had gone suddenly dry.

"It would be a pleasure," she said, stepping into his arms.

"I warn you, I am unaccustomed to dancing, especially the waltz."

"It is not so very difficult," she said, smiling up at him.

Her eyes were as blue as the aquamarine she wore around her neck. He shook himself mentally and concentrated on the steps.

They were silent for the first three turns around the room. Finally, the silence became uncomfortable, and Lady Olivia cleared her throat.

"We do not have to dance, if you would prefer to sit out quietly. I am probably making a mull of this," he said.

"No, I am enjoying myself, and you are doing very well. No one would guess you have not been practicing," she said.

"Thank you," he replied. After a moment, he said, "I suppose you like dancing very much."

"Yes, I do."

"And it is something you would not wish to give up?"

"No, I enjoy it too much—even when my partner is not as graceful as you, my lord."

"Now you are flattering me. I know there are others here who could dance circles around me. You could, I am certain."

"I suppose," she said. "But where would be the fun of that?"

"I mean, you would not wish to wed someone who could not dance with you on occasion."

Olivia's heart jumped into her throat, and she made a little strangled noise.

"This . . . this is a very strange conversation, my lord."

He seemed to brush this off and said, "I was just

wondering. Look, there is your aunt, heading to the supper room with Mr. Jenson. I was surprised to see him here."

"I told him we would be attending. I knew he had probably received an invitation. Despite the fact that he chooses not to travel in the same circles as us, he is from a good family. His father was the local squire in the village where my mother and my aunt grew up."

"He seems a very nice fellow. I thought your aunt would have an apoplexy, however, when he asked her to dance."

"He asked her to dance?"

"Indeed he did. She turned him down in no uncertain terms. I was sitting with her and could not bear the crushed look in his eyes. I got up and offered him my seat. I think they were both relieved with that solution."

"How wonderful!" said Olivia. "He comes to this ball because he knows she will be here, and then he actually asks her to dance with him. How romantic! This is progressing very nicely indeed."

"This?" asked Drew, smiling down at her. "You are not by any chance indulging in a bit of matchmaking?"

She tried to appear innocent, but the effort was too much, and she ruined the effect by giggling.

"Would it not be wonderful? I know there is some link between them in the past. She has hardly spoken to him for years, but now, she seems ready to forgive him for whatever transgression he may have committed. I think it is marvelous."

Her expression dared him to contradict her, but

he only agreed, adding, "Why should they not find each other after all these years?"

"Why not, indeed," said Olivia, her heart thumping loudly in her breast as he smiled at her again.

They finished their waltz in a companionable silence. Olivia could not remember when she had felt so comfortable while performing the waltz. Always before, she had worried that this gentleman might hold her too close or that another might not hold her tightly enough, and she would find following his lead impossible. The marquess, though his first steps had been tentative, seemed to know instinctively how to hold her and guide her. It was as if she could guess his every subtle move, and he could guess hers.

Being in his arms simply felt right. She would have loved to put her head on his shoulder. Better than that, to have kissed him again would have been heaven.

"You are flushed, are you feeling all right?"

"I . . . I am fine, my lord. As a matter of fact, I have never been better," she added, and he smiled.

CHAPTER EIGHT

The music ended and all the guests began to drift toward the dining hall where a huge buffet supper had been laid. Olivia hung back, suddenly realizing that she was on the arm of the marquess, who was sure to sit with his small band of misanthropists. What could she, the perpetual optimist, have to say to this group of disdainful fashionables?

"There is Sir Richard. Shall we join him and Lady Thorpe?" asked the marquess.

"Yes, I suppose so. I am not well acquainted with Lady Thorpe."

"You'll like Maddie. She puts up with a great deal from Richard and me, but she keeps coming back. We were all children together, you know."

"No, I didn't know," said Olivia. She allowed him to lead her toward his friends, reminding herself that she should be happy in anyone's company with the marquess by her side. When she had lied to Sir Richard about already having plans for the supper dance, she had hardly dared to hope that she would be with Drew.

"Maddie, you know Lady Olivia, do you not?"

"Certainly. Won't you be seated, my lady? I was about to send Richard off to fix me a plate. I hate being squeezed all about at these affairs, don't you? Drew, why don't you and Richard run along and get us a little something?"

When the two men had left, Olivia smiled and said, "It is a lovely ball, isn't it?"

"As balls go, I suppose. I am glad to see that your friend Lord Hardcastle finally came up to scratch. Miss Featherstone is a delightful ninny—a distant connection of mine. They should rub along very well together."

"Tony is a dear. We used to play together as children. Rather like you, Lord Sheridan, and Sir Richard."

"Not exactly, though. Although I do remember that you and Lord Hardcastle were once rumored to be . . ."

"Not at all. That was when we were both new to London. We were not seriously considering it. Do you mean that you and Lord Sheridan? . . ."

"Sheri? Goodness, no. He is by far too serious for me, always has been. No, there was a time when Richard and I talked about marriage. Still, I was destined for money, and Richard, he was mad to join the army. In the end, it came to nothing."

"But now that he is home and you are widowed?"

"No, I fear that particular flame was not strong enough to withstand the winds of time." She changed the subject and said, "I understand that you do a great deal of charity work."

Olivia raised her brows. Surely the marquess had not confided in Maddie about her visit to Vauxhall.

Cautiously, she agreed.

"There is a school, I believe."

Olivia relaxed and smiled again. "Yes, and Mr. Pendleton has agreed to give us a parcel of land so that we may move the children to a larger facility outside London."

"That is good of him. I only ask because I recently had a letter from my old governess, and she is at loose ends again. I thought if you might have a vacant post, I could write to her. She is a wonderful woman, though she is getting too old to be forever moving from place to place as her charges outgrow her."

"When we move, we are sure to need more teachers because we will have twice the space and will be seeking more children. Do write to her, and give her my direction," said Olivia.

"Your direction? I had thought to give her the address of the headmistress."

"That would be fine, too. I shall tell Mrs. Priddy about her so that she will be expecting her letter."

"You really are involved with this," said Lady Thorpe. With a frown, she added, "It makes me feel quite selfish with the little that I do."

"Not at all. I enjoy seeing the children. They are so funny. And then there is my servant, Harold. He adores the children, and they love him, too. He visits there more often than I do."

"You know, Lady Olivia, there is an interesting side to you that does not show when you are merely seen across the ballroom. It is no wonder Sheri is so wrapped up in your concerns."

Olivia's eyes opened wide, and Lady Thorpe patted her hand and said hastily, "Do not worry, my dear. I know how to keep a confidence. Besides, I only meant that Sheri has all his various charities that he supports. You two have a great deal in common. Oh, good, here are the gentlemen with our plates."

The two men set the plates down in front of the ladies. Lady Thorpe took her fork and moved something grayish brown to one side.

Her nose wrinkling in disgust, she said, "You should know better than to get me any pâté, Richard. You know I never eat goose liver."

"And I keep telling you, Maddie, you should try it. It's good."

"It is not," said Olivia. "I tasted it once, and that was all I needed."

"There, I knew the two of you would get along exceedingly well," said Sir Richard. "Now we can all be comfortable together."

"Quite comfortable," said the marquess. "Though perhaps not as comfortable as your aunt and the good doctor," he said, nodding toward a corner table where Olivia's aunt and Mr. Jenson were talking quietly.

"How lovely," said Olivia, smiling at the couple.

"Ah, love is in the air," said Sir Richard, winking at Olivia. "Just like I told you last night."

She bowed her head to hide her blush, willing him to say nothing more. Her new friend, Lady Thorpe, came to her rescue by diverting everyone's attention to the huge ice sculpture in the center of the buffet.

"That thing is decidedly lopsided, don't you think? Look, the mast is about to break off."

"It is all the candles in here," said Lord Sheridan.

"And all the people," added Olivia.

"Yes, and in a few minutes, that spear of ice is going to fall across all that beautiful food," said Sir Richard. "I wager ten guineas that it happens in the next three minutes."

The marquess laughed and said, "No, it will take longer. I say another ten minutes."

"Eight," said Lady Thorpe.

"Don't you want to place a wager, Lady Olivia?" asked Sir Richard.

"Me? I have never wagered on anything but a hand of silver loo." They all gaped at her, and she said, "Very well, I say it will take at least fifteen minutes for the ice to melt enough that the mast breaks off the ship."

"Fifteen minutes?" said Lord Sheridan. "I hope you are prepared to pay."

"And you, my lord," she replied with a smile.

Word of the wager spread to several other tables, and they all waited to see who would win. As the company began to migrate back to the ballroom, several footmen came in to straighten the buffet table. One of them reached up to remove the ice sculpture, and everyone yelled at once. The footman was so frightened that he scampered back to the kitchens empty handed.

"Twelve minutes," said the marquess. "I'm out."

"Now we have only to wait and see if the beautiful Lady Olivia will prove successful," said Sir Richard. "Three more minutes now."

Two more minutes passed, and still they waited.

"I don't think any of us are going to win," said Lady Thorpe.

"Another minute and we'll know."

There was a crackling sound, and the remaining guests in the dining room gasped. Olivia giggled.

"If anyone had told me I would be sitting here waiting on a . . . there it goes!"

The icy ship's spindly mast fell the length of the table, sending food and platters flying. Servants came running while everyone laughed.

"Shall we get back to the ballroom? I am hoping you will grant me another dance, Lady Olivia," said Sir Richard.

"Certainly," she replied.

"What about you, Maddie?" said the marquess.

"Me? I am going home. I have danced, I have played cards, and I have dined. Quite enough for one night. The three of you run along."

Sir Richard took Olivia's arm, and the marquess hesitated.

"Going to call it a night, too, old boy?" asked Sir Richard.

"No, I . . . I will stay for a little while longer," he said, following along after them.

With a glance over her shoulder, Olivia allowed Sir Richard to escort her back to the ballroom. They stood at the edge of the floor while the dancers finished the line dance they were performing. When the music began again, it was another waltz.

"I don't know if I should," said Olivia. "To dance two waltzes with the same gentleman might be considered fast."

"She has a point," said the marquess.

"Nonsense. Not when we are only friends," said Sir Richard. Still, she hung back, and he added, "We are friends, are we not, my lady?"

Looking into his eyes, Olivia couldn't help but smile. Glancing at Lord Sheridan, she said, "If you will excuse us, my lord?"

Then she placed her hand on Sir Richard's shoulder and followed his lead onto the floor.

Observing them with a sour look on his face, Drew started when Miss Hepplewhite appeared at his elbow and commented, "They make such a lovely couple."

"Do you think so?"

"Yes."

"He is a rake, you know."

"Olivia has dealt with her share of rakes and rascals," said the older woman with a laugh.

"Nevertheless, I should warn her. When she finishes this dance, I will ask her for the next and tell her just enough about Richard's reputation with the ladies to warn her."

"You may do as you wish, of course, but I do hope you plan to dance with other ladies, too."

"No, why should I wish to do that?"

Miss Hepplewhite shrugged and said, "The handsome Marquess of Sheridan attends a ball without his cane and dances for the first time in years. Once with his old friend and twice with my niece! We shall have half of London on our doorstep tomorrow, sniffing out the latest *on-dit*."

"So you are saying that in order to do what is

right by your niece, I must dance with some of these colorless young ladies."

"That is precisely what I am saying. Everyone will still be wondering why you have suddenly taken to dancing, but no one will link your name and Olivia's."

Leaning closer, he whispered, "Very well, my dear Amy, but it is only my noble and chivalrous character that is enabling me to accomplish this mission."

"*Bon chance*, Sheri," she whispered in return.

He took the hand of the first miss he came across, begging for the honor of a dance. After hasty introductions, permission was granted, and he led her onto the floor.

Drew wasted no time in maneuvering himself and his partner toward Lady Olivia and Sir Richard. She was laughing at something his friend had said. He backed his partner into another couple and threw them all a hasty apology.

Getting close to his target again, he overheard his friend say, "You cannot deny me, my lady."

"Can I not? My, but you . . ."

Other dancers came between them, and Drew ground his teeth in frustration. "Hell and blast!" he muttered.

Glancing down, he realized his partner was trembling. He apologized and spent the rest of the dance uttering trivial civilities just to appease her wounded sensibilities. After all, it wouldn't do to have it bruited about that the marquess talked to himself.

Finally, the dance was over, and Drew was able

to return the nameless miss to her chaperon. After several agonizing minutes of polite conversation, he bowed and escaped. He then tried to fight his way through the crowd to Olivia, but she was already on the floor for the next set with another partner.

Again, the marquess found another lady to partner, and then joined the square where Olivia chatted with Mr. Thomas, waiting for the musicians to begin. Drew was rehearsing what he would say to the beautiful Lady Olivia, but his partner for the quadrille was nothing like the tongue-tied miss of the previous dance. Interrupting his ruminations, she put her hand on his forearm and ran it up his sleeve with a seductive purr.

"I was hoping you would remember me," she said.

With a quick frown, he said, "Of course I remember you, Lady Givens. I knew your husband quite well. I was sorry to hear of his passing."

She shrugged and pouted at him, "I do not want to talk about him. Let us talk about you, Sheridan."

He stiffened, but she didn't appear to notice. He breathed a sigh of relief when the music started.

"Perhaps you could come by tomorrow. I am having a little gathering of friends in the afternoon."

"Hm," he said, keeping his eyes on Lady Olivia.

"I keep a very good brandy," she purred.

"Uh huh," he replied.

Finally, the steps brought him face-to-face with Lady Olivia. She smiled, and he growled.

Lifting her brows in surprise, she asked, "Whatever is the matter, my lord?"

"I have to warn you about Sir Richard."

"Warn me? Why would you need to do that?"

"You don't know him like I do. He is a rake, and . . ."

The steps required him to return her to Mr. Thomas, and he did so reluctantly. Lady Givens rattled on as they turned this way and that. The movements separated them, and Drew took a turn with one of the other ladies. Finally, he took Lady Olivia's hand again.

"You must be careful, my lady. You do not know how he can twist his words, until he has you. . . ."

With a gay laugh, Lady Olivia said, "Lord Sheridan, I assure you that I can handle Sir Richard. I know all about harmless flirtations."

Drew insisted, "Richard is not harmless."

They were separated once more. When they finally met again for a brief exchange, Drew redoubled his efforts.

"He is very adept at the art of seduction."

Again she laughed, and he wished for a moment that he could put his hands on her pretty shoulders and shake her until her teeth rattled.

"Lord Sheridan, have no fear. In truth, I look forward to my encounters with Sir Richard. What's more, I hope to be able to teach him a few lessons."

Gaping with indignation, Drew returned to his partner. One glance at his furious face, and Lady Givens fell silent. When the dance ended, Drew bowed over the lady's hand and left the ball, propelled by his insupportable fury.

If anyone had asked him, he would not have been able to express the extent of his rage. He wanted very much to throttle both his friend and the foolish Lady Olivia. There she was, a delicate flower, playing with fire. She had no sense, no common sense at all. First, it was light skirts at Vauxhall, and now rakes and seduction.

And she thought she could handle them all!

"Hell and blast!" he raged, causing his coachman to pull up and ask if he should stop.

"Good God, no! Take me home!" When the carriage was under way again, he muttered, "If I didn't have windmills in my head, I ought to have him take me all the way home to Sheridan Hall!"

Olivia fell backward onto the bed and wrapped her arms around herself. Hawkeye, who had been asleep on the pillow, sprang to his feet and hissed. When he saw the disturbance was only his mistress, he stretched and ambled closer. A wide smile on her face, Olivia turned on her side and gathered the cat close.

"You have no idea how happy I am," she said. "I know that he did not actually say anything loverlike, but he is so sweet to be concerned about Sir Richard's intentions."

"Oh, I know what you are thinking. I have had other jealous suitors, but those were just boys who fancied themselves in love with me. It is not at all the same. Though he may not be conscious of it himself, the marquess is beginning to have feelings for me—warm feelings."

She snuggled with the cat until he began to struggle. Letting him go, she sat up, blew out the candle, and climbed back into bed.

Closing her eyes, Olivia tried to sleep, but that silly grin kept her from relaxing. As the minutes ticked away toward dawn, she daydreamed about a house in the country, with the marquess and his children, and perhaps a babe in her arms.

Drew found his friend at their club, in the reading room.

"Good morning, Drew," said Sir Richard, glancing up from his newspaper.

"Good afternoon, you mean," said the marquess.

"As you wish. Do sit down. It makes a fellow feel quite insignificant having such a tall person lurking over him—rather like a predator looking down on his prey."

Drew sat down. Taking his cane, he carefully pushed aside the newspaper, causing his friend to look up in surprise.

"Did you wish to speak to me? I assure you I can listen and read at the same time. Or have you forgotten how adept I was at school, listening to the teacher at the same time I drew lewd pictures for your amusement?"

Drew couldn't help but smile, but his dark eyes grew serious again, and he said, "I want a word or two with you, and I would like your undivided attention."

Richard set aside his paper and said, "Very well. I am all attention."

"It is about Lady Olivia," said Drew, lowering his voice so that no one would hear.

"A beautiful woman but one who has been too long on the shelf. I think she is ripe for the picking."

"I know that I am not related to her in any way, but as she does not have a protector, I feel I must ask you to define your intentions toward the lady."

"Protector? A strange word to choose. Isn't that term more for a mistress and her . . . beau?"

"Never mind my terminology. Answer the question. Are your intentions honorable?"

"My intentions are my own business, but I will say this. My intentions depend entirely on the lady in question. They will be as dishonorable as she allows. And unless you plan to make her your responsibility in truth, I think you should leave well enough alone."

"Make her my responsibility? Why would I wish to do that?" asked the marquess.

"You tell me," said his friend.

"There is no need. You know how I feel about marriage. Once was more than enough for me."

"So you have always said and continue to say. However, your actions do not reflect it. So, my old friend, before you ask me to call off my pursuit of the most delightful and stunning Lady Olivia, you must decide what your interest in the lady is. Until then, I bid you good day."

Sir Richard rose and left the room. The wind taken out of his sails for the moment, Drew only sat there.

What could he say to Richard's objections? He was not ready to answer those questions. He only knew he did not want his friend to succeed.

Richard had always had the women flock to him. He was a charmer, but Drew was convinced that for Olivia, Sir Richard spelled only trouble.

He wracked his brain for some solution. After a moment, he snapped his fingers and rose, leaving the club and going home for his carriage before making his way to Lady Olivia's house.

She was out when he arrived, just as he had hoped. Instead, he asked the butler to present his card to Miss Hepplewhite. Waiting in the rose-colored drawing room, he paced back and forth.

"Lord Sheridan! What a delightful surprise! And you asked for me specifically?"

"Indeed I did," he replied, bowing over her hand. "I was hoping to have a few words with you in private. I know it is improper of me, but I would like to speak to you about your niece, and I don't want her to overhear."

"Oh, dear, Olivia is due to return at any moment. She only went to the shops for a few minutes."

"Perhaps we could go for a drive together?"

"The perfect solution," she said. "Only wait a moment while I go and put on my bonnet."

She was gone only a few minutes, but while she was out of the room, Drew heard the front door open, followed by the sound of voices.

Olivia and Sir Richard entered the drawing room.

"Good afternoon, Lord Sheridan," she said, coming up to him and giving him her hand.

She was wearing a yellow carriage dress with a floral shawl draped around her shoulders. She looked as fresh as spring.

"Good afternoon, Lady Olivia."

"Hello again, Sheri," said Sir Richard. "Wasn't it lucky of me to leave the club and run straight into Lady Olivia at the draper's?"

The marquess responded to his friend with the merest nod.

"Are you here to see me?" asked Lady Olivia.

"No, I came to take your aunt for a drive. We made plans last night," he lied. "Ah, here she is now.".

"Good afternoon, Sir Richard. How wonderful to see you again. The marquess and I were just going out, I'm afraid. I'm sure Olivia will offer you refreshments."

Drew made a choking sound and said, "Perhaps we should stay, Miss Hepplewhite. Would it be quite proper for Lady Olivia to entertain a gentleman here alone?"

Sir Richard leered at Lady Olivia, but she missed his wolfish expression as she glared at the marquess.

"Am I not visible today?" she demanded. "Why do you speak as though I were not in the room? If you wish to know what I think, then ask me."

Amy settled matters by saying, "This is all nonsense, my dear. Lord Sheridan, Olivia is past the age where one must be so very careful. Sir Richard is a gentleman, as well as a friend."

"Hear that, Sheri? I am a gentleman and a friend."

"I hope you will remember both," muttered Drew. "Very well. We should be going then. Good day, Lady Olivia."

"Good day, my lord," came the frosty reply.

When Drew had Miss Hepplewhite settled in the carriage and they were under way, he said, "The reason I am concerned about your niece, Miss Hepplewhite . . ."

"I thought I was to be called Amy when we were private."

"Very well, Amy, the reason I am concerned about your niece is Sir Richard."

"Such a delightful man. What about him?"

"He is not the saint you seem to think him."

"I never thought that he was. On the contrary, he is a great deal too amusing to be a saint. A saint would be unspeakably dull, and Sir Richard is frightfully merry. I find his company enormously amusing, and so does Olivia."

"And that is the problem. She is so busy being amused that she does not realize he is quite dangerous to her reputation."

"A rake, is he?"

"Most assuredly."

"Hm, that may not be all to the bad, Sheri. So far, Olivia has not found anyone else quite so interesting—except you, but I think she merely feels sorry for you."

"Sorry? For me?" he gasped, almost dropping the ribbons. He guided the horses through the park gates and then pulled them up short. Turning to face her, he demanded, "Why the devil would anyone feel sorry for me?"

"Let me see. You rarely smile, and you are rather silent. I mean, rumor has it that you are still grieving the loss of your wife some ten years ago."

"No, I do not smile like an idiot all the time.

And silent, I grant you that one. But let me assure you, Amy, I am not grieving over Anne. I never really did, and so you may tell everyone you know and see!"

"Please do not be angry, Sheri," she said, placing a gloved hand on his sleeve.

He covered her hand with his and then patted it. "I am not angry, just amazed at how very gullible people can be. I do not smile because I see very little to smile about—especially here in London. And to be truthful, I worry about people who smile all the time. Your niece, for example. Until getting to know her better, I thought she was nothing but a shatterbrained pea-goose, or worse—an incurable coquette. I thought it had to be one or the other the way she is always smiling and laughing at those obnoxious young coxcombs she manages to find for dancing partners."

"Olivia? I have never heard of such! She is the kindest person you will ever meet, but she is not a pea-goose or a coquette. She is really very shrewd. How else could she keep so many charities afloat?"

Drew picked up the ribbons and sent the horses along the path. "Very well. I will accept your assessment of the lady's wisdom where such matters are concerned. However, she is still an innocent, is she not?"

"An . . . of course she is!"

"Then she is no match for Richard's seductive charms."

"I think you are worrying needlessly, Sheri, but what is it you want of me?"

"I want you to let me know if she begins disappearing for hours at a time, acting secretive about her absence, and daydreaming all the time. Olivia may think he means marriage, but I must doubt it. Will you keep a watchful eye out?"

"Yes, I will do that, but I think your worries will come to nothing."

"Then you will be able to say, 'I told you so.' Until then, we will strive to keep Olivia safe."

"That is the second time you have called her simply 'Olivia,'" remarked the older woman.

"I am feeling rather like a big brother to the lady, that is all," he said gruffly. This was the second time in a matter of hours that someone had questioned his motives, and he really did not like it.

"Of course," said Amy, smiling up at him.

In the next few days, the Marquess of Sheridan marshaled his forces in his attempt to keep the Lady Olivia safe from his friend. He summoned Butters, a Bow Street Runner who often earned extra money working for him, and put him on duty, tailing his friend Sir Richard.

Miss Hepplewhite kept him informed of all of Lady Olivia's plans, and Drew appeared at every event, even two routs—though he hated every moment of them. Still, except for a bit of flirtation, Sir Richard appeared to be getting nowhere in his seduction of Lady Olivia. She was spending a great deal of time in Sir Richard's company, and this alone was enough to worry Drew. To his knowledge, however, the couple was never alone again.

After a week, Drew felt more defeated than ever. He was certain from the way Lady Olivia gazed at Sir Richard that she was falling in love with the rake. Richard was a patient man, and it was only a matter of time before he would devise a plan to get her alone.

Drew sometimes felt like he was fighting a losing battle. He also wondered why he cared. He did not for a minute think he was actually falling in love with Olivia. He remembered that feeling when, at the age of nineteen, he had fallen irrevocably for the beautiful Anne Lovelace.

Oh, the atrocious poetry he had penned! The hours spent gazing at her. He had begged for her hand the first day they met. She had laughed then and every time until the last one. She had accepted his kisses and his embraces. When her father had come to see him, to tell Drew that he would wed Anne or be shot, he had been overjoyed. He had rushed to her side only to be cursed for ruining her life.

Drew sighed at the remembrance. All Anne had ever wanted was the gaiety of London. All he had ever wanted was a simple life in the country. The marriage had been a disaster for both of them.

Unable to sleep after yet another rout that ended at four in the morning, Drew rose and dressed, walking the chilly streets until he reached the mews where Lady Olivia's horses were stabled. It was daylight, and the grooms were busy with the horses. Drew questioned several before he found the ones in charge of Lady Olivia's cattle.

"Good morning. Rattle, isn't it?"

"Aye, guvner. Wot kin I do for you?"

"I would like a word with you in private." Taking the young man aside, the marquess opened his purse. A few minutes later, he left the mews confident that he would be informed if Lady Olivia chose to go anywhere unusual.

The marquess would have felt less secure if he had heard Rattle telling his superior, Mr. Pate, about the marquess's request. Within the hour, Mr. Pate had told Harold, who digested this information and made the ponderous decision not to tell his mistress.

Later that morning, Lady Olivia met her three servants on the pavement and climbed into the closed carriage for their usual round of calls.

When she and Harold were seated and the carriage was under way, she asked, "What letter is it today, Harold?"

"What? Oh, the letter *j*."

"You seem a little distracted today," she said.

"I am, a little," he replied. "But I am ready. Let's see, for the letter *j*, besides *jar* and *jug*, which aren't very exciting, I could think only of *jab*, but when I asked Mrs. Priddy the other day, she said she didn't want me jabbing at someone. She said she would find a jack-in-the-box, whatever that is."

"It is a child's toy. I know they have one there because I gave one to little Penny. I have also seen the girls there playing jackstones. When you are teaching, you must ask the older girls to fetch a set of theirs for your lesson." A little smile on her lips, she said, "When did you see Mrs. Priddy?"

"I thought I would ask her for help with the *j*, so I stopped in."

"I see. You like Mrs. Priddy, don't you, Harold?"

"I think she is th' finest lady I have ever met—'cept for you and Miss Hepplewhite, that is."

"Well, thank you for that. And I think she is a very fine lady, too. When I was away at school, she was my teacher, you know. I thought she was the kindest lady I had ever met. When she left to marry her husband, I cried. But all's well that ends well. We kept in touch, and as it turns out, that was most fortunate for both of us. I needed someone to run my school, and she needed a purpose to go on living."

"When did her husband die, my lady?"

"It has been three years, I think."

"And she lost two babies, too?"

"Yes, they both died of the same fever."

"Such bad things shouldn't happen to such a fine lady," said Harold.

They fell silent, each lost in their own thoughts. Olivia felt a warm glow as her thoughts returned to the marquess. Drew might not be ready to declare himself, but he was definitely acting like a man in love—or very near to it. He was not being as rational as he usually was, or so Sir Richard had informed her. His friend thought it hilarious, but Olivia found it endearing.

"We're here, m'lady," said Harold, climbing down and holding out his hand for her to take.

"Good morning, my lady, Mr. Harold," said Bobby,

greeting them at the gate as usual. "Mr. Tucker is on his way with the key. He said I was to tell you."

"That's fine. How are you this morning, Bobby?"

"Fine, m'lady. And you?"

"I am quite well, thank you, sir."

The caretaker came and opened the iron gates for them to enter. The guests were running a little late, and Harold hurried ahead with the boy to begin his lesson. Olivia headed straight for her friend's office.

"Good morning, Sarah."

"Lady Olivia! Good morning. Is Harold—I mean, Mr. Hanson, with you?"

"Yes, I have sent him on to the schoolroom. He is anxious to begin his lesson."

"Oh, then I must hurry along," said the headmistress, picking up a box from the floor by her desk. "I promised that he could use Penny's jack-in-the-box for his demonstration."

"Oh, yes. I nearly forgot. I shall wait for you here." Olivia wandered around the small, neat office. There were touches here and there that made her recall the habits of her former teacher. Sarah Priddy was forever arranging her books by colors—a quirk that would drive most academicians mad. But her books, as with everything in her life, had to be pleasing aesthetically. There was symmetry, too, in the arrangement.

Between each grouping of books was a small trinket or memento. One was a miniature of her late husband, a sergeant in the Peninsular War against Napoleon. He had been killed toward the end of that war, in late 1813. This, on top of losing her twins before their first birthday, had nearly destroyed Sarah.

Someone had seen to it that Mrs. Priddy had made it back to England, and Sarah, having nowhere else to turn, had found Olivia. For a time, the bereaved widow had simply stayed with Olivia and her aunt. Finally, Sarah had decided she needed to be useful. They had hit upon the idea of the school, and Sarah Priddy had discovered a new meaning for her life, a new raison d'être.

Now, unless Olivia was wide of the mark, Sarah Priddy and her Harold were more than a little interested in each other. He was not on the same social rung, but he was a good man, and Sarah, evidently, didn't really care. What a happy ending it would be if their new school could open with the marriage of the two. Then, as Harold had so eloquently told the children only the month before, they would have a real mum and dad.

Just then, Sarah returned, her face red with the laughter that still spilled forth. "I am sorry, my dear. I just couldn't tear myself away. When I left, the bigger girls had Harold on the floor and were trying to show him how to play at jackstones. There he is with those ham-sized fists of his, trying to pick up those small figures. All the children are standing around, cheering him on."

"I should probably go and see that," said Olivia.

"In a minute. I wanted to tell you that I received that letter from Lady Thorpe's former governess. She is coming this afternoon to speak to me about a position."

"Excellent."

"Would you like to be present?"

"Heavens, no. I leave all that in your competent hands. You will know if she is right for our little school. I hope she will be. Lady Thorpe insisted that she is very kind, but it has been a number of years since Lady Thorpe was her pupil. I shall trust you in this, as always."

"Thank you, my dear. Is there anything else, or do you want to go and watch the show?"

"The show, please," laughed Olivia, following Sarah out of the office and down the hall.

They entered the schoolroom to find Harold still sitting on the floor, a child leaning over each shoulder and little Penny on his lap. He had given up on playing at jackstones, and the older girls were demonstrating the game for him. All of them were laughing and giggling. When he looked up, his smile widened, showing two rows of uneven teeth. Sarah Priddy turned pink, her gray eyes shining as she returned his gaze.

Folding her arms, Olivia smiled, too. Yes, things were working out very nicely indeed.

Reluctantly, Olivia and Harold left the school behind and continued on to the widows' home. When they arrived, Mr. Mullins greeted them with wringing hands.

"I am so glad you are here, Lady Olivia. Mrs. Tatman is gone all to pieces after receiving a most distressing letter from her mother."

"Is it one of her children?"

"Yes, they have both contracted the chicken pox, but the youngest is very ill. The doctor warns that he may not live. She is beside herself with grief and wants to go, but . . ."

"Say no more. Let me speak to her. Tell the others not to worry. I will take Mrs. Tatman with me, and put her on the stage immediately."

"Bless you, my lady," said the distraught man.

Soon, they were back in the coach, heading for the closest posting inn. Beside Olivia sat Mrs. Tatman, her eyes red from crying. She clutched her worn-out portmanteau to her bosom.

"I should have had them with me. My mum's too old to look after them right and proper."

"Now, now. You did what you thought best, Mrs. Tatman. I am sure your mother has done all she can for your sons."

"I only hope I get there in time."

The coach lurched and stopped.

"See what is the matter, Harold."

Harold hopped down and exchanged a few words with the coachman, Mr. Pate.

When he returned, he said, "It looks like a nasty snarl up ahead. Two coaches collided."

"Can we not back up and go another way?"

He glanced at their passenger and winced. "I'm afraid not, m'lady. We're blocked in. I'll see if I can go out and help th' ones behind us to back up."

Mrs. Tatman sniffled, and Olivia offered her lace handkerchief. The minutes raced past, and suddenly the door opened. The Marquess of Sheridan hopped inside.

Tipping his hat, he said, "Good afternoon, ladies."

"Lord Sheridan! I am happy you are here. We are trying to get to the George and Blue Boar Inn in Holborn. Mrs. Tatman needs to arrive in time for us to purchase a ticket for the seven-thirty P.M.

mail coach to Dover—that is, she is only going as far as Rochester. We have been sitting here for almost an hour now."

"You might be here all night, ladies. There was an accident behind you after the one in front. If you wish to take the mail, you will have to walk to the inn. However, I have my curricle waiting in the next street. I was curious what all the hubbub was about and walked through that alley to see what was going on. Then I spied your carriage, my lady. My curricle is at your disposal."

"Oh, thank you, my lord!" exclaimed Mrs. Tatman and Olivia together.

He hopped out of the carriage, and both ladies started to follow. "There is only one problem. The curricle is not large enough for three. If you wouldn't mind waiting here, Lady Olivia, I will take Mrs. Tatman up with me."

"Of course not. Go quickly, Mrs. Tatman. Here is the money for the ticket and a little extra so you may purchase something to eat."

"You are too kind, my lady!"

"Not at all. I will keep you in my prayers."

She waved, but neither Lord Sheridan nor Mrs. Tatman looked back. It was already six o'clock. They would make it if nothing else happened to delay them. For her part, she would simply have to be patient and find out what happened when next she came upon Lord Sheridan.

How wonderful that he had chanced to spy her carriage. He was a true gentleman. He might not smile all the time, but he was a noble man. He had not even questioned why she was trying to assist a commoner like Mrs. Tatman. He had not looked askance at her plain gown. He had simply stepped in and done what needed doing—rather like a knight of old.

Sitting back and allowing herself to relax, Olivia filled the remaining time with daydreams about knights and fair damsels who looked remarkably like Lord Sheridan and her.

CHAPTER NINE

Olivia arrived home in time to rush up to her room and dress. Her aunt, resplendent in her new gown of deep rose, sent her own maid to help Pansy turn out her niece in record time. Still, Olivia felt positively breathless by the time the two abigails pronounced their mistress ready to meet her guests.

Taking one last look in the glass, Olivia smiled and thanked the two maids. Her new gown was a clear blue, the color of the sky on a summer day. Silver threads had been woven into the cloth, and it shimmered in the candlelight. Her hair was piled atop her head with strands of seed pearls entwined through it. Around her neck was a single star sapphire secured on a narrow white ribbon. She had never felt more beautiful or more ready for romance.

There were some twenty people who had been invited to dine before the ball. When Olivia entered the drawing room, she spied her aunt on the sofa with Mr. Jenson on one side and Mr. Pendleton on the other, each vying for her attention. Lord

Hardcastle and Miss Featherstone were deep in conversation with her parents. Lady Thorpe and Mr. Thomas were speaking to the Grants. All this she perceived at a glance before going forward to greet these and the other guests personally.

Last came Sir Richard. Olivia had been aware that he was watching her progress around the room. She knew he was waiting for his own turn. Before she could greet Sir Richard, Witchell entered with a silver salver that contained a small card addressed to her.

Olivia opened it and found a hastily written message.

> *My dear Lady Olivia,*
> *Mrs. Tatman is safely away. I will be there for the ball, but I fear I will miss dinner.*
> *Yr Servant,*
> *Sheridan*

Peeking over her shoulder, Sir Richard said, "From Sheri, I see. Not bad news, I hope." Olivia turned to him with a brilliant smile, and he added, "I do wish he would cease being such a flat and get on with it."

"Do not be like that, Sir Richard. Lord Sheridan did a very noble thing this afternoon. Because of that, he will miss dinner, but he will be here for the ball."

"And you hope that he has somehow changed into a knowing fellow and will realize what a fool he has been. He will sweep you into his arms in a fevered frenzy and never let you go."

She did not deny it, but she giggled all the same. "The likelihood of that happening tonight is as silly as you are, my friend. Now, I am wearing a new gown tonight, and you have yet to tell me how beautiful it is. You are being quite the slowtop for a practiced rake."

If she was expecting a teasing reply, she was disappointed. The practiced rake lowered his voice to a seductive whisper and said, "I don't need to tell you how beautiful the gown is. I shall tell you simply that even as beautiful as it is, this gown is not worthy of your beauty."

Slipping the note into her reticule gave her time to decide on the proper response. With a smile, she pretended to applaud his compliment. For a brief second, a hint of pain flickered in his eyes, then it was gone. Olivia was not even certain she had seen it. He took her hand and lifted it to his lips for an impetuous kiss.

"I hope Sheri comes to his senses soon," said Sir Richard.

Giving him a sidelong glance, she asked, "Why is that?"

"If he does not, I may have to wed you myself, and that would play havoc with my reputation!"

Deciding that this conversation was becoming too dangerous, Olivia asked, "Tell me, have you seen Miss Divine yet?"

"Not yet. I left my card. Her housekeeper said she would be out of town until today."

"How very forthcoming of her to give you such personal information," teased Olivia.

"I have a way with women—some women," he corrected, giving her a speaking look.

"Here is Witchell to announce dinner," she said with relief.

Because the marquess was not present, the gentleman with the highest rank was Olivia's friend Tony, Lord Hardcastle. He left his fiancée and came forward to offer Olivia his arm. The rest of the guests found their own partners according to their own ranks. Tony led Olivia to her seat at the head of the table before going to the other end.

Mr. Pendleton, she noticed, was escorting Miss Fallon. The last couple to enter was her aunt and Mr. Jenson. Olivia smiled. Perhaps her aunt had finally decided to stop playing games with the kind doctor. Olivia certainly hoped so.

They were all seated, and the first course was served. Olivia turned to Lord Featherstone on her right and asked about the latest happenings in the House of Commons. When he had finished fifteen minutes later, Olivia spent a few minutes in conversation with Lord Grant on her left. She heard the large clock in the hallway strike the hour with ponderous precision. It seemed to mock her as she waited impatiently for Lord Sheridan's arrival.

She told herself she was being foolish, but she envisioned him dressing hurriedly, as impatient to be by her side as she was to have him there. Nonsense, of course. Most probably, Lord Sheridan was regretting the time he wasted that afternoon, executing what was, after all, her duty.

The final course was being served when Witchell leaned over her shoulder and whispered, "Lord Sheridan has arrived, my lady. As he did not wish to disturb everyone's dinner, I placed him in the drawing room."

Her mouth went suddenly dry. She half rose from her chair, then thought better of it. With what she hoped was suitable nonchalance, she announced, "I must see to another of my guests. If you will excuse me . . ."

She studiously ignored the look of amusement on Sir Richard's face and walked out of the room with decorum.

All the way down the hall, Olivia kept telling herself, *do not throw yourself at his head, do not throw yourself at his head.*

She entered the room, hand extended, and said airily, "My dear Lord Sheridan. I am so glad you were not too dreadfully inconvenienced by your good deed. Until I received your note, I was worried that you might miss the ball altogether, and I would have felt just terrible about that."

He took her hand and drew her close. For a second, she thought he meant to kiss her, and she lifted her face to his. Instead, he kissed only her hand and led her to the sofa, sitting by her side when she was comfortably situated.

"I sent the note because I didn't want you to worry—about Mrs. Tatman, I mean."

"You are too kind."

"A mere trifle," he said with a wave of his free hand. His other hand still held hers. "She told me about the home where she lives and about being away from her children."

"It is sad, I know. . . ."

"Oh, she wasn't criticizing or complaining. No, she is thankful for the opportunity you have given her."

"She is probably the most talented seamstress we have," said Olivia. "But I know it is so very difficult for her, living apart from her little ones."

"I . . . I had a thought about that. I am afraid I did not wait to discuss it with you first, my lady."

"What is it?" she asked, putting her other hand over his. The move was bold, but it was less than what she really wanted to do, which was to throw her arms about his neck in a mad embrace.

"I mentioned my own poor efforts to help our soldiers who are coming back to nothing, and I suggested that she and her children might like to move to the small village where my estate is in Hampshire. Our seamstress fell ill last spring and has had to retire. Mrs. Tatman could find plenty of work to make ends meet, and I would be happy to supply her with a house."

"What a wonderful idea!" said Olivia, patting his hand vigorously.

He leaned closer, his dark eyes warm and inviting. She tilted her head in anticipation.

"Olivia, the other guests are beginning to arrive," hissed her aunt from the doorway.

The marquess rose and held out his hand to help Olivia to her feet. With a sigh, Olivia stood and took his arm, going out to greet her guests with a frustrated heart.

Drew sought out his friend Lady Thorpe to watch the dancing. Olivia was standing with her aunt to greet the guests as they arrived. His lips twitched as he watched Olivia's gown sway back and forth with each movement.

"What are you laughing about?" asked Maddie.

"Nothing. Just Lady Olivia over there, tapping her foot in time to the music."

"That is a very pretty gown she is wearing. I must remember to ask her who made it up for her. I could not wear that color, but the style is nice."

"She should always wear blue, particularly that shade," he said before squirming with embarrassment.

Maddie took pity on him and pretended not to notice. Sir Richard, who had been flitting from one small group to another, finally sauntered up to speak to them.

"You are very busy tonight, Richard," said Maddie.

"Just securing a dance with each of the prettiest girls in the room. Except you, of course, dear Maddie, unless you would care to? . . ."

"I am not dancing tonight."

"I cannot credit it," said Richard. "Surely just one dance with me?"

"No, Richard. That is how it all starts. I prefer to sit out with Drew for the evening."

"Sit out with . . . my dear lady, there is no guarantee that our formerly taciturn Sheri will actually be sitting out. He has become quite the favorite with the doting mamas in the past week. I cannot quite fathom his sudden penchant for dancing with jittery young ladies, but I have seen it occur so often of late, I can only assume he is hanging out for a young wife."

"Rubbish," said Drew, his nose high and his gaze never leaving the dancers.

"Then you are not dancing tonight?" asked Richard.

Drew looked his old friend square in the face and said, "I will demmed well do as I please without any of your speculations or nonsense. Would you care to take a stroll in the garden, Maddie?"

"Of course, Sheri. Perhaps later," she said to Richard, her expression perplexed.

When they reached the high terrace that overlooked the garden, Drew hesitated. "It is too chilly for a proper stroll in that gown of yours, Maddie. Why don't we simply sit on that bench in the corner on the terrace?"

"Very well," she said, already clinging to him for warmth against the cool breeze. "What has gotten into you and Richard of late? I would suspect you two of a feud if I did not know you better. You never get truly angry."

"No, but I am rather disgusted by the attention Richard is lavishing on Lady Olivia. If he meant marriage, it would be different, but you and I both know that is not the case."

"And why does it disgust you so?" she asked.

"My opinion of him has suffered, I can tell you."

"And your opinion of Lady Olivia? I mean, if she is encouraging him . . ."

"She is not!" he exclaimed. "That is, I would not call it encouraging. She is certainly friendly, but then she has always been friendly, you know that."

"Yes, I do seem to recall that her smile was the one thing that made you doubt her good sense. What has happened to alter that opinion?"

"Alter? I don't know. Perhaps I have thought twice about the foolish things I have said about Lady Olivia. In truth, she is a fine lady, a lady of great sensibilities and goodness. If she has one fault, she is perhaps a little too kind."

Maddie giggled, and she snuggled against his coat for warmth. "Such admiration," she said. "One would almost think that you are in love with her."

"In love? Me? Now you have gone mad! I admire her. I applaud her good works, but I am . . . not . . . no, I cannot be in love. I was cured of that particular ailment when I was a bridegroom of nineteen."

"Of course," said his friend. After a moment, she said, "Drew, have you ever wondered what would have become of you if you had not fallen head over ears in love with Anne? Would you be so bitter about love?"

"I have never told anyone this, though you might have guessed. I was not in love with Anne, not by the time we married. I had already seen through her, but it was too late. Rebekah was on the way, so I did the honorable thing."

"I had guessed," said Maddie. "But Drew, is that any reason to spend a lifetime alone, refusing to admit that your feelings do exist?"

"This from you, Maddie? You, who have vowed never to wed again?"

"That is entirely different," she said with a laugh. Rising, she said, "Take me inside, you brute! I am freezing out here." With Maddie still clinging to him, they strolled back into the ballroom just as Lady Olivia turned from her post to smile at the multitude of people who had come to her ball.

Her eyes met Drew's, and he smiled at her. Her face shone with delight, and he was drawn back to Maddie's words—was the past any reason to spend the rest of his life alone?

He looked down at his arm and gently disengaged himself from his friend. "If you will excuse me, Maddie?"

"Certainly, Sheri," she said, sending him off with a little push. "Good luck."

Olivia left her aunt's side and stepped into the ballroom. He knew she was coming to him, to talk with him, to dance with him—anything he chose to offer. His chest swelled as his heart was gripped by some undefined emotion.

"Lord Sherida . . ."

He ignored the voice. He ignored the smiles of recognition and greeting as he crossed the crowded room. He ignored everything but her. Olivia. Coming to him.

He saw Sir Richard put his hand on Olivia's arm, and she stopped.

Drew stopped, too, his heart in his throat.

Though she glanced in his direction, she nodded to his friend and took his arm, allowing him to lead her away from Drew and off the dance floor.

Drew growled, "Hell and blast!"

The young lady next to him gasped and moved away, but Drew didn't care. He seethed with anger and jealousy as he watched Richard bend his head to Olivia's.

After a moment, the marquess realized she was not going to tear away from Sir Richard and fly into his own arms. His anger melted into misery, and he left the ballroom and the house, not even stopping for his carriage. He walked through the streets to his town house and proceeded to get roaring drunk—all alone.

* *# *

Five minutes passed before Olivia thought about the marquess and returned to the ballroom. Spying Lady Thorpe, she approached her on the pretense of telling her that her former governess was as good as hired at the school. Then, very casually, Olivia asked where Lord Sheridan had gone.

"Gone? I have no idea. He was with me one minute and then he bolted. I thought he was going to speak to you, my dear."

"Oh, well, I am certain he is here someplace. I hope you enjoy yourself," said Olivia.

"I shall. I am just on my way to sit with your aunt. She is always such a delight to listen to. A woman of great good sense."

It took Olivia only a few minutes to scour the various spots where the marquess might be lingering. Determining that he had left without a word, a slow heat began to burn.

Olivia knew that something had gone terribly wrong, but she was also very put out by the marquess's odd departure. Surely he had not been that jealous. She would not have gone with Sir Richard if he had not shown her the message his servant had brought, telling him that they could meet the very next day with Miss Divine. Excited to have her new project finally under way, Olivia had babbled on about what they would accomplish for these unfortunate members of the demimonde.

She had thought, foolish female that she was, that when their eyes had met across the floor, Lord Sheridan had been intent on her. Obviously, she had completely misread his silent message. Or perhaps he had not even been looking at her. For all she knew, he might have been staring at someone or something behind her.

The concept that Lord Sheridan might have been staring at some other lady with that single-minded intensity sent a flame of jealousy raging through her. How dare he! And who? Who else could he . . . Olivia took a deep breath. Now who was being unreasonable? She could not rebuke him for leaving in a huff of jealousy when her own was out of control.

No, it was merely a misunderstanding—something they could fix and then laugh about. She would have to be patient until she saw him again. On this sane thought, Olivia acknowledged the young man asking for the pleasure of a dance and allowed him to lead her onto the floor.

Although her ball had not gone precisely as planned, she would not allow herself to consider it a complete disaster.

At the least, she now knew he truly cared for her. He hadn't said it, but the admiration in his eyes and his manner of speaking to her in the drawing room were proof enough.

And for the moment, she told herself firmly, she would have to be satisfied.

"My lord, Mr. Fitzsimmons has requested your presence in the study. Mr. Butters is with him."

If Drew's valet's voice made him groan, the curtains being opened to allow the morning sun inside made him dive under the covers again.

"Go away."

"Certainly, my lord, but Mr. Fitzsimmons said to tell you that it was very important."

Drew threw the pillow off his head and sat up. He regretted it instantly as a wave of pain resonated in his head and a violent upheaval tore at his stomach.

Holding out one hand, he said, "Get me . . ."

"Here, my lord," said Fenwick, handing him a small glass with clear liquid.

Drew downed it in a gulp and then waited. After a moment, he nodded. The pain in his head was still there, but he no longer felt in need of a bucket.

"Coffee, my lord?"

"Not yet, just get me my dressing gown. I'll be demmed if I'll go to the trouble of dressing for this."

"Very good, my lord," said Fenwick, easing his master into a brocade dressing gown. "If I could just . . ." The valet sighed and put the brush back on the dressing table while the marquess strode out of the room.

When Drew entered the study, he headed straight for the sideboard and the tray of decanters. Pouring a small quantity of brandy, he turned to face his secretary and the Bow Street Runner.

"Good morning, my lord," said Fitzsimmons. When the marquess said nothing, he continued. "Mr. Butters has some good news."

"Well, out with it."

"It's like this, my lord. I haven't seen the subject with any ladies in the past week. He has been to a Miss Divine's house several times, but as far as I can ascertain, she has never been at home."

"Evelina Divine?" asked the marquess. "Why the deuce would Richard go there? She's under the protection of Pinchot."

"As I said, my lord, she is not home anyway, and he never stays more than a few minutes. I supposed that it was one of the maids or the housekeeper that interested him, but they are all too old and ugly."

"There's been no one else?"

"No, my lord." The Bow Street Runner flipped open a small notebook and said, "He's been driving twice with that Lady Olivia. And he has called there two . . . no, three times."

"Ah ha!"

"No, my lord. There have always been others present. The drawing room draperies were open, and I could tell there were a number of people inside."

"I don't understand. He must be slipping away when you are unaware."

"Not a chance. I've got someone watching his rooms all night long, and I'm there all day."

"Where else does he go?"

"He has gone to his tailor, to Tattersall's, to Jackson's Boxing Salon twice, and he's out in the evening all hours, but there are hundreds of people at those affairs. He goes to his club each morning for breakfast. Oh, and he also frequents a small coffeehouse off of Piccadilly. I followed him inside, but he was just sitting there, having a cup of coffee."

"This is all very frustrating. Butters, he has to be meeting my lady friend somewhere."

"Perhaps, sir, it would be better if you told me the name of your lady friend and I followed her."

Drew waved his hand and said, "As you have probably guessed, the lady in question is Lady Olivia Cunningham, but there is no need. I have bribed her tiger to let me know if she goes anywhere untoward."

The Runner dug his foot into the carpet before clearing his throat to say, "If you'll forgive me for sayin' it, my lord, perhaps her servant is not being completely truthful with you."

"Well, of course he . . ." Drew's indignation faded as the Runner continued.

"I understand she has a reputation as a very kind lady. When I asked the footman near the front door about his mistress, he told me to . . . well, he did not give me any information about the lady and that is unusual. Most of 'em will spill the soup for only a bob or two."

"I see. Yes, you are probably right, Butters. No doubt her tiger simply pocketed the coins and has said nothing."

"So do you want me to switch and keep an eye on Lady Olivia?"

"Yes, but finish out this day with Sir Richard. Tomorrow you can switch to Lady Olivia for a couple of days. After that, if there is nothing to report, then I will simply call it off."

"Very good, my lord." The short, little man gave a stiff bow and left them.

The dedicated secretary cleared his throat.

"You can speak, Fitz. We have been together too long for you to worry that I will be offended," said Drew.

"I was just wondering why you are so certain that there is anything havey-cavey going on between Sir Richard and Lady Olivia Cunningham?"

Drew gave a mirthless chuckle. After a moment, he said, "I am not certain, but I want to be sure before I make another mistake in marrying."

The secretary gasped in surprise, and Drew gave a dry chuckle.

"I am not ready to declare myself. I mean to say, I might not be so fortunate this time as I was the last . . . Devil take me. I don't mean that. Losing the mother of my children was tragic. And though my wife despised the country life I required, she was a good mother to Rebekah. If she had lived, she would have been a good mother to Arthur, too. Heaven knows, the boy needs someone else to appreciate the things he enjoys."

"I would not worry about the young earl, my lord. Just because he prefers reading about horses to riding them does not mean he will not be a satisfactory marquess one day. The scientific aspect of farming should intrigue him, and he has a very quick mind."

"Thank you, Fitz. I can see that Arthur does have at least one ally at home."

"You are his best ally, my lord."

"I try, I just don't seem to understand him very well. But never mind. First, I need to sort out this other matter."

"Can I do anything to help, my lord?"

"You are already doing everything you can by taking care of all the other details of my life. Thank you. You are more than just a secretary, Fitz. You are a friend." Drew extended his hand, and the blushing secretary shook it.

"Thank you, my lord."

"I am going out to my club now. If Butters should happen to return with news . . ."

"I will send for you immediately."

Drew strolled out the door, feeling very much more the thing. His stomach had settled down, and the aching in his head was growing dull. He had not done that in years—drowning his sorrows. Now he remembered why. It would not happen again.

Olivia climbed into the closed coach, and they were off. The coach moved slowly through the busy streets, carrying her to the small coffeehouse off Piccadilly Street.

The butterflies that occupied her stomach took flight as the group neared its destination. Except for those few encounters at Vauxhall, Olivia had never spoken to, or even been in the same room, as someone's mistress. And Evelina Divine had evidently been at her position—did one call it that, she wondered—for a very long time.

The carriage stopped, and Harold got out. Rattle climbed off the back of the carriage and kept an eye out, too. After looking up and down the street, Harold offered his hand to help Olivia descend. Pulling a veil over her face, Olivia hopped down.

"Wait here, Rattle," she whispered, then laughed nervously at herself for acting so secretive. "Harold, come in with me and guard the door to the parlor."

Inside, she nodded to the owner who cocked his head toward a door at the back of the room. Olivia hurried through the quiet coffeehouse and opened the rear door.

Sir Richard ushered her inside and closed the door. "Good morning, my lady. May I present Evelina Divine?"

Olivia had the immediate impression that this was a lady, not someone's mistress. On closer inspection, Olivia could see that the woman was made up and that her clothes were perhaps a little too revealing. Other than that, she could have passed for a member of the *ton*.

"Good morning, Miss Divine," said Olivia.

"And Evelina, this is Lady Olivia," said Sir Richard.

"Good morning, my lady," said the red-headed woman in cultured tones. Olivia must have looked surprised, for Evelina added, "I used to be on the stage. Accent work was my specialty."

"I see. I am so pleased you agreed to meet with me, Miss Divine. I hope the time was not inconvenient," said Olivia, taking the seat Sir Richard offered.

"Not at all. Dear Richard has always been so very persuasive," she said with a leer that caused Olivia to blush and stare at him.

"It was nothing," he said, using his finger to loosen his constrictive cravat. "I told her basically what you want to do, Olivia, but you will have to explain the details."

"I am only too happy to do so," said Olivia, losing all her nervousness as she warmed to her theme. "Sir Richard has most likely explained that I want to help girls who have fallen on hard times, who have been forced into . . . prostitution," she said, managing not to blush at this forthright speech.

"Not all of these girls have been forced," said the hardened mistress.

"Not forced? But . . . oh, I see what you mean. Very well, I want to offer these girls help. Whether they take my help is their own choice."

This seemed to satisfy Miss Divine because she nodded and said, "There are some who never get used to it. They are the ones who could use your help. Them and the ones who are fresh from the country, looking for a new, exciting life here in London."

"Yes, yes, that is exactly the type of girl I want to help. I had asked Sir Richard if going to a brothel . . ."

"You, my lady? In a brothel?" The light skirt was clearly shocked. "No, you mustn't consider it. Why, you, an unmarried lady in a brothel? It is unthinkable."

"Then will you help?"

Miss Divine considered it for a moment and then said, "I will help, but I am not going into any brothels either. No, what we want is to beat the old abbess at her own game."

"Abbess?"

"What they call the woman who runs the brothel," said Sir Richard.

"Some of them have people who scout the posting inns around London, looking for fresh faces from the country. If a girl arrives and there's no one to greet her, these so-called gentlemen offer their help. Before she knows it, the girl has been taken to a fancy house."

"How dreadful," murmured Olivia. "What happens next?"

Evelina Divine was not as naive as her listener, and she looked to Sir Richard for guidance. When he nodded, she continued.

"Sometimes they are drugged. Sometimes they are whipped into submission, but submit they must. As virgins, they are sold to the highest bidder."

Olivia shivered, her heart going out to these victims. "We must help them," she said quietly. "What do we do first?"

"First, I will send an agent out to see which inns would be the best locations to send our own scouts. While we are waiting for his report, you will need to figure out what we will do with the girls when and if they decide to accept your help."

Olivia smiled and said, "I have already purchased another house and have had it cleaned top to bottom. There are five large rooms with four beds in each one. I have hired two former housekeepers to instruct the girls in service, if that is what they want. If they prefer learning a trade such as sewing, I have people who would be willing to do that."

"You are a wonder," said Miss Divine.

"I could do all this, and it would be for nothing without your help, Miss Divine. Together, we will make a formidable team."

"Call me Evelina, my lady."

"Thank you."

"I think we should call it a day," said Sir Richard.

"Very well. Will you check to make sure it is safe

for me to go out through the front? You had best knock to get out of the room. I left Harold standing guard outside the door," said Olivia.

He left them alone, and Olivia said, "If I can do anything for you, Evelina . . ."

The woman laughed, the sound soft and inviting. She shook her head and said, "Goodness no, my lady. I have no need of your help. I am quite content the way things stand for me."

"But do you not want to be . . . free?"

"My lady, I am free. I haven't a care in the world."

"But some day, surely, you will tire of this life. It cannot be pleasant to be the subject of someone else's whims."

"You have this all wrong. I know I am not a proper lady like you, but I command a great deal of respect. I can come and go as I please. I was gone this past week to Paris."

"By yourself?"

"Yes, by myself," she said with another laugh. "My sister lives there, and I paid her a visit. I have been home two days—by myself."

"But what if your . . . protector tires of you?"

"He will not be the first. But I have my own house and my own carriage and jewels. And they are real," she added, lifting the heavy gold necklace with its rubies and diamonds. "Can you say the same?"

Olivia, who wore only a simple strand of pearls, smiled. "Yes, these are, but I know many people wear paste when they go out because they are afraid to lose their real jewels."

"You see, I don't have that worry. If these should be stolen or lost, I will simply ask for more. So please, my lady, if we are to get on, you mustn't try to right the wrongs in my life. I would only be annoyed."

Olivia chuckled and promised to limit her crusade to the innocents.

"When can we meet again?" she asked.

"Thursday morning? I would like to see the facility you have, if you don't mind. We could meet and go from here. After that, I may even have other news by then."

"Thursday morning is fine with me."

"What time?"

"At eleven o'clock," said Olivia. "If you should need to change it, just send a note to Sir Richard. He has agreed to be our go-between."

"I am amazed that you managed to persuade him to help," said Evelina. "In my experience, Sir Richard Adair has always been singularly unhelpful. I have never known him to go out of his way when there was nothing in it for him."

"I merely asked."

"Ah, I see how things stand," said the woman of the world.

Olivia giggled and hastened to say, "No, it is nothing like that. As a matter of fact, there is someone else who . . . but I do not wish to say too much on that head. I thought Sir Richard agreed because of you."

"Me? No, there is nothing like that between the handsome Sir Richard and me. Whatever his reasons, I am glad he thought to approach me. I think I will enjoy our little enterprise."

"I am glad. It has already been quite an education for me. Here I was thinking an abbess was like a mother superior." They shared a laugh. Then Olivia sobered and said, "Evelina, thank you."

"You are quite welcome. Good day, my lady."

Richard opened the door and signaled to Olivia that it was safe to leave. She pulled her veil into place and left the private parlor. With a wave to Miss Divine, Sir Richard followed Olivia out of the coffeehouse and into her carriage.

"What do you think of Evelina?" he asked when they were under way.

"I think she is a godsend, Sir Richard. Thank you for finding her."

"You are very welcome, my lady. Now, can I tempt you with an ice from Gunter's?"

"No, I have an appointment with my hairdresser. Shall we drop you someplace?"

"In the park. There I should be able to blend in. Wouldn't do to simply get out anywhere, not when we have been in a closed carriage together."

"Yes, just the three of us," said Olivia, glancing at the opposite seat where Harold was watching the practiced rake with a wary eye.

"I see what you mean. Nevertheless, I think the park would be the best place to discharge me."

"Have you seen Lord Sheridan this morning?"

"No, I haven't. Have you?" he teased.

"You know I have not. I was a little worried about him. He disappeared quite early last night without saying good-bye."

"Sheri was ever a peculiar sort," he replied, twitching the curtain back from the window to see where they were. "He is spying on me, you know."

"What? Why on earth would he do such a non-sensical thing?"

"Probably because he is insanely jealous over you, my dear Lady Olivia, and he thinks that I am out to seduce you."

"Ridiculous!"

"Thank you so much," he replied.

"Oh, you know what I mean, and I cannot believe it. Why would he think such a thing?" she asked.

Richard grinned and said, "Possibly because I admitted as much to him myself?"

"I think it is all a hum. You are making it up. Besides, why wouldn't he have people spying on me, too?" she asked.

Harold cleared his throat.

Frowning, Olivia demanded, "What do you know about this, Harold?"

"I believe his lordship made an attempt to spy upon you, my lady. Fortunately, he chose to bribe Rattle, who told Mr. Pate immediately. Mr. Pate told me about it, but there didn't seem to be any reason to raise a fuss over it as none of us would ever betray you, my lady."

"I am surrounded by intrigue," she muttered. "Why did you not tell me?"

"We didn't want to worry you none."

"So he is spying on me, too! I have a good mind to demand an explanation! I think I will have Mr. Pate turn this carriage around and go straight to Lord Sheridan's house!"

"No!" exclaimed both men at once.

"Listen, Olivia, you don't need an explanation. I mean, can you not guess why? Sheri is a fool, but he is a fool in love."

"I cannot credit it. Why would he not just come right out and tell me?"

"We are talking about the same marquess, are we not?" asked Sir Richard. "The one I am talking about married when he was little more than a boy, only to regret it since the day it occurred. I am talking about the one who has sworn never to have anything to do with another woman as long as he lives."

"Then how can he possibly be . . . you know."

"You have only to look in a mirror for the answer to that."

"What drivel you do spout, Richard!"

"Drivel? I give you a lovely compliment, and this is the thanks I get. I am immeasurably hurt," he put a limp hand to his forehead.

"Pray, do not be silly. Very well, thank you, but please do not continue to practice your flirting on me. You know it hasn't the slightest effect—except, perhaps, to annoy me."

"Point taken."

"So if I cannot confront my Lord Sheridan, then what am I to do?"

"Nothing. He will soon realize the error of his ways."

"And that is?"

"That you and I are not, alas, having an affair, not even a minor one. You will forgive him for being a complete flat, and you and he will do the happily-ever-after thing like in the fairy tales."

She heaved a doubtful sigh.

"Have faith," he whispered, tapping on the roof to ask Mr. Pate to stop the carriage. "Will I see you tomorrow?"

"No, I am spending the day with a friend in Islington who is in her confinement."

"Until Thursday at eleven then," said Sir Richard, blowing her a kiss before leaping nimbly to the ground.

Olivia hardly noticed his departure, she was so wrapped up in her thoughts about Lord Sheridan. She smiled and wondered what she would call him. Sheri? My lord? Or simply Drew. Yes, that was the one. It felt so right to think of him in those terms.

She frowned. If only he were not such a paper skull, they could be planning their nuptials at that very moment. All this, of course, if Sir Richard was right.

Oh, how she hoped he was right.

CHAPTER TEN

"I have no desire to lounge about on the grass and ruin my new gown," grumbled Lady Thorpe, squinting up at the bright blue sky.

"Now, Maddie, we must enter into the spirit of Pendleton's alfresco breakfast," said Drew, offering his arm.

Lady Thorpe put up her parasol, and they walked to the back of the Italian-style villa, following the red carpet that had been unfurled on the grass.

"I do not understand this penchant people have for dining out of doors. The only thing I want to do out of doors is go for a drive—and that, through a civilized park. This business of living in the wilds . . ."

"Richmond is hardly the wilds," said Drew with a chuckle. "Pendleton has all the comfort of living in the country, but he is close to London. Not a bad arrangement, if one is forced to endure the rigors of the Season. I might consider it myself when

Rebekah has her Season. Perhaps my mother might even be persuaded to come."

The house itself stood on a small rise and the green lawns sloped gently to the bank of the Thames. To the left, a large tent in green-and-white stripes had been erected.

"A spectacular view," said Drew, feeling his cares slip away as the scene filled his soul, sending him back home again.

His companion was less than enthused and said, "I can see that you will be positively repulsive all day in your gentleman farmer guise. I am going to find a glass of something to dull my senses."

Maddie left him there, and Drew wandered down to the lawn where other guests reclined on the grass on blankets or sat at one of the small tables that dotted the landscape. On the river, several energetic guests were rowing small boats while a few were punting. One small group played at shuttlecocks, and yet another played croquet. Under the tent were the older guests. Sofas and chairs had been arranged in clusters as if they were inside a drawing room.

Not recognizing any particular friends, Drew followed Maddie toward the tent. There, he fell into conversation with his host, who was holding court with eight or ten older ladies. When Drew spied Miss Hepplewhite enter, he turned away. Until he had a report from Butters, he had vowed that he would avoid Lady Olivia and that meant avoiding her aunt, too.

Miss Hepplewhite had seen him, however, and was coming to speak to him. He could not very well give her the cut direct.

Miss Hepplewhite announced, "Lord Sheridan, I am so happy to see you. Where have you been of late? You should come to call more often, like your friend Sir Richard."

His hackles raised, Drew gave a cold shrug. "Unlike my here-and-there friend, I have business to attend to, estates to see to. I cannot be forever languishing over some pretty face."

"My, we have got a bee in our bonnet," she said, taking his arm and practically dragging him away from the others. When they were seated on a small sofa together, she said, "Now, tell Amy all about it. Have you had a quarrel with your friend?"

"Miss Hepplewhite, I . . ."

"Oh, this is dire indeed if I am once again Miss Hepplewhite. Have I managed to offend you, too? Have I?"

Since she would not leave well enough alone, he said, "No, you have done nothing. I am annoyed with your niece and my friend, and it is churlish of me to take it out on you. I humbly apologize."

"Oh good. Then we can be friends, but I take it you do not wish to divulge what sin Olivia and Richard . . . oh!" she exclaimed, and he could feel his face turning red. "But my dear Sheri, what can you expect when you have not made the least attempt. . . ." His darkling glance silenced her.

"I know that she is unaware of my . . . regard. She is practically unaware of me."

"No, I assure you that she is aware of you, but perhaps not in the manner you would like. Dearie me, this is a dilemma."

Drew managed a smile and said, "Not at all. I am

not one to throw myself at a female. I will simply bow out."

"It might be for the best. Mind you, Olivia does not appear to me to be interested in Sir Richard in that manner, though she has been spending a great deal of time with him. And he is charming. There is no denying that."

"Never mind," came his flat comment. "We still have each other, you and I. Unless your good doctor is lurking about in one of the corners."

"No, he had patients to see, drat the man."

"So, are you going to put him out of his misery?" asked Drew.

"I have not decided yet. It will not be anytime soon, I can tell you. I have waited a lifetime. I can wait a bit longer. Now, enough of this depressing tattle," said Miss Hepplewhite, getting on her feet and taking his arm.

Glancing up at him, she said, "Shall we stroll on the lawn and laugh at all the young men making cakes of themselves over the ladies? If we are lucky, perhaps one of them will actually fall in the water."

"I am at your service," he replied. They wandered away from the tent, their path taking them ever closer to the river.

"Only look at that young man trying to punt along the shore." They watched the youth push away from shore with a long pole, leaning out farther and farther as the boat slipped away.

"If he is not careful, he's going to come a cropper," said Drew.

Amy laughed and said, "Why, I think it is Mr. Campion. I am surprised his mother is not sitting between him and the young lady. Oh, dear. Look how the boat is wobbling."

Drew chuckled and pointed to the long, narrow punt. "So it is, and I fear young Mr. Campion is not content with only upsetting his own boat.

"Look out!" called Drew, running toward the shore as the young man managed to pluck the long pole out of the mud, losing control as it flew overhead. It fell with a resounding crack across the bow of another punt.

Her voice shrill, Amy shouted, "Sir Richard! Watch out!"

It was too late. Sir Richard, who was standing in the other punt, lost his balance. Clinging to his pole, the punt shot out from under him. While he held onto the pole, the punt rammed the shore, sending its lone passenger into the shallow water.

"Olivia!" screamed Amy.

Drew plunged into the chest-high water and gathered Olivia into his arms. Richard finally let go of the pole and stood up, sloshing through the water to shore.

"Of all the ham-fisted things to do," snapped Drew.

"Are you speaking to me?" demanded Olivia while she struggled to get free.

"No, I am speaking to that gudgeon there," said the marquess, depositing her on the shore with a grunt. He turned to help his friend out of the water. "Letting a little pole upset you. You've lost your touch."

"At least I once had a touch. You don't go near the things because you know you will end in the river."

"One time!" shouted Drew, beginning to enjoy himself.

"One time you would admit to. What about when you took your fancy piece . . . but I am forgetting myself. Are you all right, Olivia?"

Servants with blankets rushed up, wrapping the warm woolen cloths around their shoulders, but Drew didn't notice. Richard's use of Olivia's given name made Drew remember his complaint with his friend. "If you will excuse me."

He turned away as Olivia said, "Drew," but people were crowding about them, and the disgruntled marquess didn't hear.

"Leave him be," said Richard, tugging on her arm to lead her to the house. "There is time enough to worry about him. At the moment he is too jealous of me to see reason."

"I begin to doubt it, Richard," she whispered.

"Then you must try harder to believe me. Let him stew in his own juices a few more days. Then, when he decides it is time to make his declaration, you can tell him what a lobcock he has been. Trust me on this."

"I am trying to, Richard, but it is becoming more and more difficult. The hurt in his eyes when he saw me in the boat with you—it was almost unbearable."

While servants were dispatched to their various houses for clean clothes, Drew, Olivia, and Sir Richard waited in separate bedrooms. Hot baths were drawn. Afterward, they each sat in borrowed dressing gowns, waiting for their clothing to arrive.

Being the restless sort, Sir Richard was soon fidgeting with knickknacks, staring out the window, and finally, opening his door to see if he had heard someone in the hall.

"Damn," he muttered. A door opened, and he pulled his to, peering through the narrow aperture.

"Will there be anything else, m'lady?" asked a maid as she left the room next door.

Richard waited for the maid to leave, and then he tiptoed down the hall. A gentle knock brought a muffled, "Come in."

He pushed open the door and entered, shutting it silently behind him.

"What is . . . Sir Richard!" gasped Olivia. Clutching the loose neckline of her dressing gown, she said, "I thought the maid was returning. What are you doing in here?"

"I was bored. Do you have any cards? We could play a hand of piquet to pass the time." As he spoke, he wandered toward her, looking about him.

"Certainly not!" she said, backing toward the bed as he came closer. This was a tactical error, she quickly realized, and began to back toward the door to the adjoining room. Was she fast enough to zip through the door and lock it from the other side?

Stopping, he gave a quiet laugh. "Surely you are not afraid of me, are you?"

"Not afraid," she breathed. "But how would it look to anyone coming in? You don't wish to compromise me, do you?"

"Who would come in?"

"My aunt, for one," said Olivia, still edging toward the door.

"I just spied her down by the river talking to Maddie. Look, no one is going to find out. I am bored," he whined. "I need someone to entertain me."

"If you think Lady Olivia is going to entertain you, Richard, you will have to come through me first."

For the first time in her life, Olivia swooned. The marquess, slipping inside the room from his adjoining one, caught her handily before she hit the floor.

"Now see what you have done," said Drew, carrying her easily to the bed and laying her on it. He tucked her dressing gown around her legs. Looking at her pale face, he smoothed some blond tendrils of hair from her brow before turning to his friend.

Richard was still chuckling as he said, "Me? She was quite conscious when she was speaking to me. You are the one who caused her to faint. Bully!"

Drew, however, was deadly serious when he said, "Get out, Richard, before I call you out."

Richard fell silent. His nostrils flared and his lip curled. He glanced away. When he looked back, the usual gleam was in his eyes and he said, "I would not accept, Drew, and you know it. I would be signing my own death warrant because I would refuse to fight, and you would have to kill me. Then you would be put to death, and it would be such a terribly messy affair. Neither of us wants that. Why don't you go back where you came from, and I will do the same? No one will be hurt."

"Go on. I'll leave when I have made certain she is unharmed."

Richard shrugged and backed out of the room.

Drew heaved a sigh of relief. His friend might be a rogue, but he was still a man of honor and occasional good sense. Richard was wrong about one thing, however. Drew knew he would never have been able to fire either.

He went to the basin and wet a cloth. Returning to Olivia, he began bathing her face.

The foolish smile faded, and the marquess cursed himself for a fool. What was he doing? Was his first forced marriage not enough? All he needed was to compromise Olivia and force her to wed him. She would not be with child like Anne had been, but if someone discovered him in her room, both of them half dressed, the result would be the same.

Besides, he asked himself, *am I really so sure that she was backing away from Richard?* Perhaps she was merely going to check to see that the door to his room was locked.

No, that couldn't be it. She had looked afraid. But of whom? asked a little voice inside.

"She called me Drew," he replied.

And she called him Richard earlier, said that malicious voice.

"Hell and blast," the marquess muttered through clenched teeth.

Olivia's eyes fluttered and opened. She caught his hand and tried to sit up. He pushed her down gently.

"It was not what you thought, Drew."

"I am certain of that," he assured her. "Are you all right?"

"Yes, I . . . I don't know what came over me."

"The shock of seeing me in your chamber, no doubt." He handed her the cloth and walked across the room to the adjoining door. "Don't worry, I will leave you alone now."

"But Drew . . ."

"Rest well," he said, going through the door. Glancing back, he gave her a quick smile and shut the door.

Olivia jumped off the bed and then grabbed the table to steady herself as the room began to spin. Taking even breaths, she walked slowly to the door and opened it.

Crossing the room to the fire where he sat, she stood before the marquess, her hands on her hips. Mustering all her frustration and anger, she snapped, "You are the rudest man I have ever encountered!"

"In what way?" he said calmly, his very composure fueling the flames of her anger.

"You know very well, in what way! I told you nothing happened between me and Sir Richard, and you didn't believe me."

"If I recall correctly, I did say that I believed you, my lady."

"And that is another thing. Why is it Richard calls me Olivia, but you do not?"

He actually smiled at this, reached out, and took her hand. He held it in his, turning the palm up and tracing her lifeline. She shivered.

"Am I to be judged by Richard's standards?" he

said, his voice so soft and seductive, she forgot to breathe.

Olivia felt light-headed again and looked for someplace to sit down. He sensed her need and took her onto his lap. It seemed the most natural thing in the world to put her head on his shoulder.

"Am I?" he whispered.

"No," she replied, her breath coming in short rasps as he took her chin and lifted it to meet his kiss.

Slow and deep, stirring her soul, robbing her mind of any thought except the hope that it would continue. Hands moving and touching, thrilling her body in a way . . .

"I came at once, my lord!" exclaimed Fenwick as he opened the hallway door and minced across the room carrying one of Drew's coats above his head.

Olivia leapt up and stumbled toward the adjoining door. She was gone before anyone else entered the room.

"Hell and blast," murmured the marquess.

One of the footmen followed, laden with a bandbox that he placed on the bed. Fenwick placed the coat on the bed, smoothing every crease. Opening the bandbox, he began pulling out several choices of waistcoats, shirts, and numerous cravats.

He paused in his unpacking and glanced at the marquess. The valet looked at the borrowed dressing gown and clutched his throat, saying, "Please tell me, my lord, that you removed the merino coat before you plunged into the murky depths of the river."

"I'm afraid not. Sorry, Fenwick," said Drew.

The valet shuddered and shook his head mournfully. "You will be careful with your new waistcoat, will you not, my lord? It arrived this morning after you had gone, and I thought it would be quite suitable for this afternoon's breakfast."

"It is fine, Fenwick. Can we just dispense with the fashion lecture and get on with it?"

"Lecture, why, I would never presume to lecture you, my lord," said the valet. "I only wished to make certain that the clothes I brought were pleasing to you. I try my best. . . ."

After several more minutes in this vein, Drew threw up his hands. "All right, all right. I am sorry, Fenwick. I never meant to wound your delicate sensibilities. I merely want to dress and rejoin the rest of the company before it is time to go home again."

"Very good, my lord," said the sullen valet, quickly finishing his task and pronouncing his master fit for viewing.

"Thank you, Fenwick. A splendid job, as usual. And thank you for getting here in such a timely fashion."

"You are most welcome, my lord," said the valet, brushing at a speck of dust when his master walked past him on the way to the door.

"Come along, Olivia. Mr. Jenson has surprised me and driven all the way out here for the evening. He has asked me if I might waltz with him. He has been taking lessons to please me, you know."

"How kind of him, Aunt," said Olivia. "Um, do you know how to waltz?"

"Of course, I practiced it several times, and how difficult can it be when your partner guides you through it."

"Not too difficult, I hope," said Olivia, managing to refrain from uttering the nervous giggle that was begging to escape.

By now, they were at the top landing of the stairs. Olivia put out a hand to stop her aunt.

"I don't know if I can do this," she whispered.

"Not go through with it? Rubbish! Of course you can go through with it. You are not some milk-and-water miss to be vanquished by a couple of men. Besides, you should be flattered to have two such handsome men fighting over you."

"They are not fighting *over* me so much as . . . oh, I don't know. At times, I would like to horse-whip both of them!"

"If you ask me, the marquess . . ."

Two ladies passed them on the stairs, and Olivia and her aunt remained silent until they were alone again.

Olivia waved her fan to cool her heated face as she recalled that kiss. She had thought the kiss they shared at Vauxhall was breathless. She hadn't realized a kiss could make one absolutely mindless.

"So what are you going to do?"

Olivia smiled and shook her head. "I grant you, he is maddening, Aunt, but oh, when he smiles . . ."

"I smile, you smile, everyone smiles, my dear child. Calm yourself."

"I know, I know," she said, taking a deep breath and beginning the too-short descent.

"There is Charles," whispered her aunt. "You will be all right?"

Olivia nodded and gave her aunt's hand a squeeze. Then she was alone, poised to enter this ballroom by herself. Never had she felt so unsure of herself.

"May I have the pleasure of sitting with you while you wait for the next dance, my lady?" asked the boring Mr. Campion.

"Certainly," she replied and took his arm.

He led her to a small alcove where they sat down on a small sofa.

"I wanted to apologize for upsetting your friend's punt. I did not spend a great deal of time practicing such sports when I was at university."

"Do not trouble yourself about that, Mr. Campion. None of us came to any lasting harm," she said, hoping that was all he was going to say. Oh, to sit there quietly with her thoughts, but it was not to be.

Mr. Campion liked the sound of his own voice very much, and he proceeded to drone on about boats and steam engines for the next ten minutes. Every once in a great while, he required some response. Being the good listener that she was, Olivia paid enough attention to fill these short gaps.

The music ended, and Tony asked for the honor of that waltz. Olivia was glad. If it had been Sir Richard, she would have been tempted to turn him down, especially with the marquess watching. Now that she thought about it, she couldn't recall seeing Drew since he had come into her room.

As the evening progressed, Olivia felt her nerves

were being stretched to the limit. Drew never left the dance floor, but he never approached her. Had their kiss given him a disgust of her? She prayed it had not. She certainly had not felt one iota of disgust—only raw passion.

Waltzes, cotillions, quadrilles. All passed without the marquess approaching her. Finally, she sat out one dance with Mr. Pendleton. The music ended, and the old man rose to speak to other guests.

When a shadow fell across her lap, Olivia glanced up and drew in a quick breath.

"Good evening, Lady Olivia."

"Good evening, Lord Sheridan," said Olivia. She knew she was smiling like a looby, but she could not stop herself.

"Lady Olivia, might I have the next dance?"

She smiled up at him and held out her hand. Rising, she followed Drew onto the floor.

"It's about time," she whispered as his hand clasped hers and his other arm encircled her.

"Yes, old Pendleton is a nice enough fellow, but after sitting out with him for a whole dance . . ."

"Not because of that," she said with a carefree laugh. "Quite true, of course, but what I meant to say was, I wanted to explain about this afternoon, Drew. I didn't get the chance when I came into your room." She blushed at the remembrance of what she had done in that room.

"Shh, not now. I am counting the beats."

She glared at him. There was no reason for him to count beats. He was now quite accomplished at the waltz. He was merely doing this to avoid conversation with her.

"Here we go. One . . . two . . . three. One . . . two . . . three."

Shaking her head at this nonsense, she said, "You are not going to allow me to explain, are you?"

"No. I might not like your explanation, and that would put me in an abysmal mood, so I think we should not speak of it at all. Well, would you look at that? How wonderful!" he exclaimed, nodding to her aunt and the doctor as they struggled by in each other's arms.

"How do you make this look so easy?" demanded Miss Hepplewhite.

Drew shrugged, and the older couple lumbered off.

Olivia giggled.

"Shame on you for laughing at their efforts, my lady."

"I cannot help it. He has taken perhaps two lessons. My aunt has only tried it once or twice. How could she have thought it would be easy?"

"I applaud them for trying it," he said, leaning closer to her as he spoke. "Bravo for them."

Olivia could not tear her eyes away from his. She wanted to speak but had lost the ability. The afternoon's fiasco with Richard stood between them. Their passionate kiss stood between them. Until she explained . . . and now she could not find the words.

"Breathe," he whispered.

She gulped down some air and said suddenly, "It was not what it looked like. I mean, me and Sir Richard."

"I never dreamed that it was," he said, smiling now.

Olivia returned that smile and inched closer as their dance continued.

"You are not angry?"

There was that smile again. "No, I don't believe I am," he said, his dark eyes gleaming with mischief.

Olivia frowned and said, "What happened to Sir Richard? I haven't seen him all evening."

The marquess tried to look innocent, but he couldn't fool Olivia, and she said, "You did not fight, did you?"

"Certainly not, I merely suggested that Fenwick, my valet, might wish to help Sir Richard because he was not feeling well."

"And how did he help Richard?" she asked.

"Richard couldn't sleep, and Fenwick happened to have some laudanum in his bag. He merely . . ."

"That is too bad of you, Drew!"

He smiled again and said, "Call me Drew again, and you may scold me all you wish."

"Drew," she whispered, returning that wonderful smile.

Too soon, it was over, and they promenaded with the other couples. Her hand was tucked into his arm, and he kept her close. When their walk was done, he bowed over her hand.

"Until tomorrow," he said, kissing her fingertips.

"You are leaving?" she said.

"I hope you will forgive me. I cannot imagine dancing with another after you." He walked away.

"But we could . . ." Olivia's voice dwindled to nothing.

"Lady Olivia, would you care to dance?" asked Mr. Thomas.

"Certainly, Mr. uh. . . ," she said.

"Thomas," he supplied.

"Of course, I beg your pardon. My mind was wandering. I believe you asked me to dance?" she said, taking his arm.

Her smile made Mr. Thomas forget everything else, and while she continued fooling the world that she was enjoying herself, Olivia was longing for only one pair of arms to hold her, to guide her in the dance of love.

After seeking out his host to bid him farewell, Drew climbed into his carriage and returned to London. He was surprised at his lightheartedness, and he knew his waltz with Olivia was responsible for it—that and the passionate interlude they had shared. People would be talking about their waltz though—the fact that he had danced only once, and with Lady Olivia.

If he had seen Richard before leaving, he would have snapped his fingers at him. He felt suddenly confident that he had nothing to fear from his old friend.

Drew dozed as the carriage swayed back and forth, its springs protecting him from uncomfortable bumps.

When the door opened and the footman thrust a lamp toward the opening, Drew awoke and stretched. Climbing down, he walked up the steps and entered the house.

"Good evening, my lord," said Silvers with a slight bow.

"Silvers."

"We were not expecting you to be this early, my lord. Mr. Fenwick told us that it was going to be quite an extravagant affair."

"And so it was, but I did not feel like staying," said Drew, picking up a letter from the side table.

"That arrived while you were gone this afternoon, my lord. Mr. Butters gave it to Mr. Fitzsimmons. He said I should give it to you immediately when you returned. My lord, is anything the matter?" asked the butler.

Drew crumpled the letter in his fist. "No, nothing. I . . . good night, Silvers."

"Good night, my lord," said the butler.

With a weary tread, Drew climbed the stairs to his room. He tore off his cravat and shrugged out of his coat before Fenwick found him and completed the job. Dressed for bed, Drew glanced down at the crumpled paper he still clutched in his hand.

Smoothing it out, he held it up to the fire and read it again.

The lady in question went to the same coffee-house as the gentleman did. She took him up in her carriage. According to the landlord, the gentleman has reserved the private parlor for tomorrow at eleven.
Butters

Drew pitched the paper into the fire where it flamed brightly and was consumed.

The feeling of betrayal was overwhelming. He had been so sure, so very sure. And now . . . but Butters didn't make mistakes.

Too weary to utter his usual curse, Drew climbed into bed and quickly fell asleep.

CHAPTER ELEVEN

Floating on a rosy cloud of hope, Olivia awoke the next morning a few minutes before the clock chimed the hour of ten. Both she and Hawkeye, who had been napping on her bed, stretched languorously. Olivia then hopped out of bed, her spirits soaring.

He had danced only with her last night. This interesting fact had traveled the length and breadth of Mr. Pendleton's ballroom. Speculation was rife, and Olivia was delighted with each rumor as it came to rest in her ears.

"What a glorious day we have in front of us," she said to Hawkeye. He looked at her and then proceeded to clean his paw.

"First, I will meet with Evelina to show her the building and find out which posting inns would be the most productive for our little project. Then tonight, we have the card party at the Davidsons', and guess what? Letitia Davidson confided in me that Drew has accepted their invitation, too." Olivia did a little pirouette and hugged herself.

"But first, my dear fellow, we have work to do."

She pulled the rope for her maid. A moment later, Pansy entered, carrying a tray with some toast and coffee.

"Good morning, my lady."

"Good morning, Pansy. Sunshine again today, I think."

"I think so. That's what Mr. Pate says. Which dress for this morning, my lady?"

"Make it the green crepe carriage dress, Pansy. I have a mind to look my best. It is one of those days that feels like it will be full of good fortune, and I want to be suitably dressed."

"Very good, my lady."

An hour later, Olivia was waiting near the front door for her carriage to arrive. Glancing out the window, she spied a little man watching the house. One of the marquess's henchmen. Olivia smiled. Then she frowned.

Why was the man there? Surely the marquess would have called him off after their intensely intimate kiss the previous evening. It was quite obvious, however, that he had not done so.

Perhaps her dear Drew had forgotten. Or perhaps . . . yes, that must be it. The man had not reported for the day, and Drew had not yet had a chance to tell him there was no longer a need to watch her.

Convinced that this was the most probable explanation, Olivia was tempted to go outside and tell the man herself. Just then, her carriage rolled to a stop at the front door. Olivia left the house and entered the carriage with Harold climbing in after her.

"Good morning, Harold," she said.

"Good morning, m'lady."

They started off, and Olivia frowned, looking at her servant's hand for the book he was currently reading.

He noticed her puzzled look and said, "I don't have a book with me because I . . . I wanted to talk to you about something, my lady, with your permission."

"Certainly, Harold. What is it?"

"I went to the school yesterday morning, my lady."

When he didn't continue, she prompted him by asking, "How is everyone? All well, I hope."

"Oh, yes, my lady. There is nothing the matter with the school. No, it was . . . me."

"What happened, Harold? Did you get the children too excited with your lesson? Were the boys too rambunctious?"

"No, nothing like that. No, I have been visiting it whenever I have a bit o' free time. I knew you wouldn't mind, and . . ."

Leaning across the seat, she covered his large hand with hers and gave it a squeeze. "You can tell me anything, Harold."

He raised his weathered face and a tear slipped down his cheek. "It's Mrs. Priddy. I . . . I kissed her hand. I didn't plan on it, but I did. I was afraid she was going to . . ."

"I'm sorry, Harold. You must understand, she has been through so much. She didn't mean to hurt your feelings."

"She didn't hurt me, my lady," he said, awe and wonder in his wide blue eyes. "She kissed my cheek."

"Sarah? I mean, Mrs. Priddy? She kissed you?"

"Yes, my lady. You could have knocked me over with a feather, you could. What does it mean, my lady?"

"I'm not certain I know," she replied.

"I never dreamed that she might return my . . . regard. But if she does, it would be the most wonderful thing!"

"Didn't you ask her?"

"No, my lady. I simply left her office and went home. I didn't know what to do or say."

"But Harold, you should have said something!" exclaimed Olivia. Men! Were they all so dense?

"I know," he moaned. "She must hate me now."

"No, she may think you are fickle, but if I know my Mrs. Priddy, and I do, she is wishing she had not kissed your cheek. She is wondering why she did such a forward thing. And she probably wants to die all over again."

"No! She mustn't wish that! I couldn't bear it!"

"Then we must go there at once so that you may tell her. We should have just enough time. Mr. Pate!" she called.

The carriage stopped, Harold swung out to give the driver the change in orders, and they turned at the next street.

When the carriage rolled to a stop in front of the school, the gentle giant said, "What do I say to her?"

"I don't know, Harold. That is for you to decide. I will tell you this, if you and Sarah should want to marry, you will make the perfect caretaker of the new school."

"And I can still teach the little 'uns their letters?"

"If the headmistress says so," replied Olivia, grinning down at him. "I will stay here. You should go in alone."

"But my lady . . ."

"Go. Be brave. Be bold."

"Yes, my lady."

The carriage door closed, and Olivia said, "And be quick about it." Olivia closed her eyes and tried to be patient.

Not ten minutes later, the carriage door was thrown open, and Harold climbed inside.

"What happened?"

"She forgave me, my lady."

"And?"

"And she said I should come by on Sunday to escort her and the children to services."

He beamed, and Olivia smiled. Sarah had always been the cautious sort. Perhaps by the time the new school was open, she would grant Harold her hand in marriage.

If anyone tried to force her to such patience, thought Olivia, she would have their heads on a platter. At this ridiculous thought, she smiled again.

If she could have moved time any faster, she would have—to that night at the card party when she would see his dear face again. She would do much more than simply kiss his cheek. This thought made her face flame, but she pulled down the veil so that her servant could not see. They were almost at the coffeehouse anyway.

It troubled her, all this secrecy, but her reputation would be in shreds if anyone discovered she was associating with the likes of Evelina Divine. Not to mention meeting Sir Richard in a private parlor. But now, she wanted to tell Drew. Surely he would understand why she was doing it. After all, he was the one who had made her promise not to hunt for light skirts at Vauxhall. Surely he would not want to deny her wish to help those unfortunate girls.

"We're almost there, my lady," announced Harold.

Having Mr. Pate circle around to the back of the building, Evelina Divine and Sir Richard slipped inside with no one the wiser. Harold climbed up beside the driver, and they were away.

Their short journey took them to the building where Olivia wanted to house the girls that they managed to rescue.

As they neared their destination, Olivia said, "Evelina, I have asked Mrs. Miller to be present at the building to show you where the girls will live and work."

"Good, I think I can be more convincing if I know what the girls are getting for their cooperation."

"Certainly," said Olivia. She was really warming up to this woman of the world. It surprised her, but then, she had never had any trouble finding the good in people.

The carriage stopped, and Harold climbed down and opened the door. Sitting in the rear-facing seat, Richard gave a succinct curse and pulled the door closed again.

"Did you see him?"

"Who?"

"The man who has been watching me for the past week. I don't understand. He wasn't following me earlier on the way to the coffeehouse. I looked for him. I thought Drew must have given up."

"He is not following you. He is following me," said Olivia. "He was outside the house when I left. But how did he get to the coffeehouse? He didn't have a hackney cab waiting, and we went by the school first."

"Who is this man?" asked Evelina.

"One of my friends doesn't trust me with Lady Olivia. He is having both of us watched—though they are making a rather poor job of it."

"I still don't understand," said the courtesan.

"It is nothing," replied Olivia. "Sir Richard is trying to make intrigue where there is nothing but childish jealousy. It doesn't matter anymore, Richard. Let us go inside."

"You two go on. I'm going to stay right here, out of sight. I know you will think I am being cowardly, but I have no desire to have Sheri call me out. If all the man has to report is that he saw you and Evelina entering a building . . ."

"Then stay. We are going inside."

Olivia opened the door while Sir Richard moved to the corner of the carriage.

"Really, Sir Richard. It is ridiculous of you to act like this. Lord Sheridan would never call you out."

"You think not? When we were twelve, he took a whip to me for whipping my own horse. If he thought I had had my way with you, Olivia, he would not hesitate . . . close the door, for heaven's sake!"

After Mrs. Miller had shown Evelina the building and the courtesan had asked dozens of questions, Evelina and Olivia returned to the carriage where Sir Richard waited, seated on the floor.

"Good heavens, Richard. The man is not going to eat you."

Climbing back onto the seat, Richard said, "I keep telling you. It's not him I'm afraid of."

"I still say Lord Sheridan would never—"

"Look, can we just go back to the coffeehouse?"

Harold closed the carriage door and climbed up to sit beside Mr. Pate. They began the short journey back to the coffeehouse.

"Can't you tell him to go faster? The man is on foot. You ladies can finish your business, and we can all be out of the private parlor before he ever gets back."

Olivia called out, "Spring 'em, Mr. Pate," and the carriage picked up speed.

Back at the coffeehouse, they entered through the front door. As before, Richard accompanied the two ladies into the private parlor while Harold stood guard at the door.

Drew stepped into his carriage with a heavy heart. He had almost decided to remain at home. If Lady Olivia had chosen to ruin herself with his friend, then so be it.

But at the last minute, he had ordered his curricle brought 'round. Driving his restive team kept his mind occupied, but he was decidedly glum. His tiger, hanging onto the back, let loose a string of expletives when Drew nearly hit another carriage.

"Enough of that, Ned. No need to burn the ears of half of London."

"Better t' burn their ears than to run them down, m'lord," said the cheeky boy.

"Shaddup," growled the marquess.

Olivia and Richard. The thought kept going around and around in his brain, making it impossible to concentrate on his driving—or anything else, for that matter.

"That's th' one yer lookin' fer, m'lord," said the tiger.

Drew pulled on the ribbons, bringing his grays to a halt. Ned ran to their heads while Drew climbed down.

"This shouldn't take too long, Ned."

He glanced at the carriage ahead of him and frowned. The tiger waiting beside it was undoubtedly Olivia's groom. So Butters had been right. Nothing but an illicit affair could bring Olivia to such a common place.

The thought made his blood boil. The lethargy that had led him to doubt whether he should even go to the coffeehouse fled, replaced by a rising storm of fury.

He stalked to the coffeehouse door. Olivia's tiger glanced at him as he passed. Then the youth shot past, running inside just before Drew.

"It's him!" he said to the giant guarding the door to the private parlor.

"Hello," said Drew, his hand forming a fist. "Harold, isn't it? I'm going in there."

"No, m'lord. You are not," said the giant.

"Yes, I am. Get out of my way!" Drew shoved the giant's shoulder, but he was immovable. He let go a blow to the giant's stomach, but it had almost no effect.

Drew grabbed Harold by the shoulders and pushed him to one side. Harold took the marquess's arm and shoved him away. Drew staggered and fell against a table. Shaking his head to clear it, he charged, his head crashing against Harold's stomach.

The big man said, "Ooof!" and doubled over. Seeing his chance, Drew rammed his fist into that big nose. The giant groaned and crumpled.

The parlor door opened, and Olivia demanded, "What in the world is going on?" Glancing at her servant, she turned to the marquess and, as Harold later told the children, she bunged him one in the eye.

He grabbed her wrists and set her aside, his fury turned to his rival now who was still inside the parlor, laughing at them.

With a primal growl, Drew lunged for Richard, catching him by surprise. Richard threw a punch that sent him reeling, but Drew came back and planted him a facer, despite the small fury hanging onto his arm, trying to drag him back.

"Stop! Stop! Drew, have you lost your mind?" screeched Olivia.

"Good afternoon, Lord Sheridan," said a calm, feminine voice.

Drew dropped his hand, spinning around to face Evelina Divine. Harold, who was on his feet again, shut the door on the coffeehouse's interested customers.

Grabbing the back of the nearest chair, Drew sagged against it, glancing at Miss Divine, then Richard, and finally Olivia, who gave him a tremulous smile.

Sitting down, he said, "What the devil is going on?"

After smoothing her gown and catching her breath, Olivia said, "Miss Divine and I have joined forces. We plan to save country girls who arrive in London without any funds from the horrors of the brothel. Miss Divine has devised a plan to seek them out, and I have purchased a building where they may live and learn a trade."

"And Richard?"

"Just helping out, old boy. When Olivia needed help, she turned to me."

This made Drew groan, but he said nothing.

"Come on, Evelina. I think the two of us are decidedly de trop." Richard opened the door that led to the alleyway behind the coffeehouse, and the worldly Evelina followed him outside.

"Come here," said Drew, opening his arms to Olivia.

She gave him a timid smile and allowed him to pull her onto his lap. He bowed his head so that their foreheads touched.

"Why Richard? Why did you not come to me?" Drew asked

"I couldn't, not after the way you behaved at Vauxhall."

"But you know I am very involved in my own charity work." He raised his head and stared at her. "You didn't think you could trust me. You might be right. I would probably have become all starchy about you associating with any of these women, even one as kind as Evelina Divine. I still don't see how you managed to persuade Richard. He is not known for his benevolence."

"No, but when he realized I was not at all interested in him, but in someone else entirely, we became friends. He knew Evelina, of course, and enlisted her help. And I think we will be wildly successful, Drew," she added, hugging his neck in her enthusiasm.

He smiled, and she sighed, gazing at him with those wide blue eyes.

"I have only one other question, my dear Olivia. Who is it that has captured your heart?"

Putting her arms around his neck, she kissed him. He pulled her close, responding to her lips like a man starved of all affection for a lifetime—as indeed he almost had been.

Several minutes passed in this pleasurable manner, but Drew finally broke it off.

With a devilish grin, he asked, "You didn't answer me. Who is this man who has captured your heart?"

Olivia pretended to slap his face. Drew winced when her hand touched his swollen cheek.

"Oh, Drew, forgive me," she breathed, replacing her hand with her lips.

When he had had another portion of her sweet passion, he leaned back again.

"I will forgive you everything, for a forfeit, my dearest love."

"What is that, my lord?" she asked, wiggling in his lap until he held her still.

"Your forfeit is that you will marry me as quickly as is humanly possible."

"Are you certain, Drew? I love you to distraction, but do you love me enough to forget the past?"

"What past? I can only think of my future now, and if you are not in it, then it doesn't exist. I love you with all my heart. Will you marry me?"

"Oh yes, my darling Drew! I thought you would never ask!"

ABOUT THE AUTHOR

Julia Parks lives in Texas with her husband of thirty-three years. She teaches high school French and loves traveling to Europe with her students and family. When not teaching or writing, she enjoys playing with her grandchildren, quilting, and reading.

She appreciates comments from her readers and hopes you will contact her through Zebra Books or via e-mail at dendonbell@netscape.net.

BOOK YOUR PLACE ON OUR WEBSITE AND MAKE THE READING CONNECTION!

We've created a customized website just for our very special readers, where you can get the inside scoop on everything that's going on with Zebra, Pinnacle and Kensington books.

When you come online, you'll have the exciting opportunity to:

- View covers of upcoming books
- Read sample chapters
- Learn about our future publishing schedule (listed by publication month *and author*)
- Find out when your favorite authors will be visiting a city near you
- Search for and order backlist books from our online catalog
- Check out author bios and background information
- Send e-mail to your favorite authors
- Meet the Kensington staff online
- Join us in weekly chats with authors, readers and other guests
- Get writing guidelines
- AND MUCH MORE!

**Visit our website at
http://www.kensingtonbooks.com**